P9-CEM-733

Praise for Barbara Delinsky

"Delinsky is an expert at portraying strong women characters."

Booklist

"Delinsky is one of those writers who knows how to introduce characters to her readers in such a way that they become more like old friends than works of fiction."

Flint Journal

"Delinsky is an engaging writer who knows how to interweave several stories about complex relationships and keep her books interesting to the end. Her special talent for description gives the reader almost virtual references to the surroundings she creates."

Newark Star Ledger

"Delinsky's prose is spare, controlled and poignant as she evokes the simplicity and joys of small-town life."

Publishers Weekly

"Delinsky steers clear of treacle . . . with simple prose and a deliberate avoidance of happily-ever-after clichés."

People

"Delinsky should touch even the most jaded of readers."

Chattanooga Times

"Delinsky creates . . . a remarkably beautiful story."

Baton Rouge Advocate

Books by Barbara Delinsky

Shades of Grace
Together Alone
For My Daughters
Suddenly
More Than Friends
A Woman Betrayed
Finger Prints
Within Reach
The Passions of Chelsea Kane
The Carpenter's Lady
Gemstone
Variation on a Theme
Passion and Illusion
An Irresistible Impulse
Fast Courting
Search for a New Dawn
Sensuous Burgundy
A Time to Love
Moment to Moment
Rekindled
Sweet Ember
A Woman's Place

BARBARA DELINSKY

Moment To Moment

HarperTorch
An Imprint of HarperCollinsPublishers

A paperback edition of this book was published in 1984 by Dell Publishing Co., under the pseudonym Bonnie Drake.

HARPERTORCH
An Imprint of HarperCollins*Publishers*
10 East 53rd Street
New York, New York 10022-5299

First HarperTorch paperback printing: September 2004
First HarperCollins paperback printing: January 1998

HarperCollins®, HarperTorch™, and ❦™ are trademarks of HarperCollins Publishers Inc.

Printed in the United States of America

Visit HarperTorch on the World Wide Web at www.harpercollins.com

30 29 28 27 26 25 24 23 22

To Kathy,
who really did it!

Moment To
Moment

ONE

She'd had far too many attacks in her life not to know what was happening. Staggering to a large rock by the side of the road, Dana fumbled with the zippered pocket of her Windbreaker, finally managing to extract the small inhalator she always carried. Exhaling as far as her laboring lungs would allow, she raised the mouthpiece, breathed in, and squeezed. Twice she repeated the procedure. Then, propped against the rock, she waited for the wheezing to ease.

Strangely, she was less worried about her lungs than she was about the cold. Having been running for twenty minutes, she'd built up a sweat that was well apt to chill her as she sat still. Her watch, its face narrowly framed between her Windbreaker cuff and the top of her wool gloves, told her it was nearly five. She looked up and around. Five o'clock and the roadway was dark. But then, it was the middle of winter. The days were shorter. It had been dusk when she'd left the house. As for the traffic, or more correctly the lack of it, could she expect otherwise on New Year's Day? The townsfolk would be in their homes, or in those of their neighbors or relatives, finishing off the last of their turkey dinners, if not already hooked by the endless string of football games the day offered.

Not Dana Madison. She'd had enough. Four hours at her parents' house had drawn her patience to its limits.

It had started when she'd first stepped foot inside the door carrying a sweet potato and apple casserole. Her mother had glared at it, appalled. "Why did you do this, Dana? I thought I told you not to worry, that I'd take care of everything."

"It's just a casserole, Mother. I may have spent all of half an hour making it."

"Half an hour when you could have been resting," the older woman chided her gently. "You shouldn't have done it."

Dana had gritted her teeth then, for the first of many times that afternoon. "Well, it's done. Will you take it?"

4

For an instant she'd half wondered if her offering would be refused. But while her mother was grossly overprotective, she was neither rude nor insensitive. "Of course, dear," she'd said, taking the casserole. "Now, you go sit in the living room and relax. I'll call your father in from the yard. Max and the others will be here any minute."

"Let me give you a hand in the kitch—"

"No, no. You sit." The pointing finger was one Dana knew well. It had been a major reason she'd finally moved out of her parents' house nearly four years before. In her private scheme of things, there were too many better out-lets for her energy than arguing with that finger.

And so she had sunk into the living room chair in which it seemed she'd spent half of her childhood. Within minutes her father had appeared at the door, wiping his hands on a dishtowel.

"Dana! Hi, sweetheart!" He'd burst into a smile and had covered the space to the armchair in which Dana was ensconced before she'd even been able to uncross her legs. Leaning down, he kissed her warmly. "How are you? Feeling all right?"

His stance was unsettling. With his hands

propped on the arms of her chair, he was her jailor. She couldn't move. Suppressing an urge to scream, she'd managed to force a smile. 'I'm fine, Dad.' She glanced at the towel he'd slung over one shoulder and attempted to change the subject. "You've been cutting wood?"

"Greasing the chain saw," he'd responded absently. His attention was elsewhere. "You look too thin."

"I look fine."

"Have you lost more weight?"

"Dad, I was chubby before. I'm in far better shape without those extra fifteen pounds."

"You were in good shape before."

She'd sighed. It could have been a replay of a tape made the week before, on Christmas Day. What her father—what her *parents*—thought of her weight, her health, her job, her running, was irrelevant. Her life was her own now. She knew that.

"Look, let's not argue," she'd pleaded softly. Despite the strides she'd made in the last few years, arguing remained against her nature. "It's the holiday. I'm here. I feel wonderful. And, for the first time in my life, I'm proud of the way I look. Now"—she cocked a mocking brow—"are you going to be pleasant . . . or am I going to get up and sprint five times around the house?"

"You're *still* running? Dana, I thought we told you—"

She'd sobered then. "Dad! I'm a grown woman. It's *my* life!"

If the firmness of her tone had momentarily put him down, it didn't keep him down long. When her brother, Max, arrived with his wife and three children, her father brought up the issue of weight again, soliciting Max's support in a futile bid to bring Dana to her senses. When their neighbors, the Holtzmans, arrived and dared to compliment her on how lovely she looked, Dana suspected her father would have liked to turn them out there and then.

And it went on through dinner, not only from her father, but from her mother and Max and Max's wife as well. If it wasn't, "Is that all you're having, Dana? Here, have a little more. It's good for you," it was "No, Dana, don't get up. Alexis will help me clear, won't you, Alexis?" Or "Jimmy, don't hang on Aunt Dana like that. It's a strain on her."

Dana calmly overlooked the fact that her wineglass was filled only halfway, and even then not replenished when her father made second rounds with the bottle. She patiently ignored the slow study of her undertaken by each of her parents in turn, then the concerned glances they exchanged. But when her mother launched into a repeat of "Are you sure you're feeling all right? You look a little pale," she could bear no more.

"If I'm pale," she said quietly, her blue eyes flashing, "it's simply to accommodate you all. Honestly, I think you'd feel *more* comfortable if I started to gasp!"

"That's a horrible thing to say," her father had countered with a frown, and she'd felt instantly contrite.

"I know. But I do think that way sometimes. Seriously, Dad, I feel better than I ever have. I have my own apartment, my own job, my own friends—friends, many of whom, by the way, don't even know I'm an asthmatic."

"But *we* know," her mother broke in, "and we worry. Can you really fault us for that? It's bad enough that you're living all alone. You should be with people who can care for you."

"I'm a big girl, Mother. I can care for myself!" she'd answered in frustration.

"Through an attack?"

"I'll have you know that I haven't had an

attack in months. But, yes, I have handled myself through one—and survived." She'd turned apologetically to the Holtzmans. "I'm sorry you have to listen to this. We have a . . . difference of opinion."

"You *were* a sick child," Louis Holtzman had interjected gently. He and his wife, Marsha, had lived next to the Madisons for more than thirty years. They clearly recalled the day Dana had been born. "We *all* worried."

"Well," she'd said with a sigh of defeat, "I'm fine now. And I'd personally much rather hear about Max's case than my own." Her senior by eight years, Max was one of the state's prominent assistant district attorneys. He had just won a verdict on an explosive bribery and conspiracy case which, mercifully, he was willing and able to discuss.

The conversation had switched tracks for a while then, even taking several further detours with the progression of the meal. As Dana had known would happen though, the state of her health was far from forgotten.

"Have you seen Chip lately?" her mother asked hesitantly when the two of them sat over a last cup of tea after the others had left the table. Chip Wilson was the allergist who'd been treating Dana for years. That he'd become a friend of the family was natural, but awkward for Dana. In explaining her bid for independence to him, she'd made it clear that from that point on he'd be dealing with her, and not her parents. Her mother was fit to be tied.

"Uh-huh. I saw him last summer."

"Last *summer?* But you should see him once a month!"

"Not if I'm perfectly well."

"You do look too thin. Your father's right. Are they working you too hard?"

"I work in a library, Mother. What quieter job could you ask for?"

"You don't lift books, do you?"

And so it had gone on, with Dana struggling to remain patient. But the strain had taken its toll. With pleas of fatigue which were instantly accepted, if not applauded, she took her leave at four and headed for her own place, ducking inside only long enough to change into her running clothes before hitting the streets.

Freedom. That was what running meant to her. It was the wind against her face, the road beneath her foot. It was a sense of power, a control of the passage of time and space. It was the unification of mind and body—something she'd never before achieved.

But now she sat, hunched over on a rock, trying desperately to catch the breath that swollen air pipes denied her lungs. If anything, she wheezed more loudly than she had moments before. And she knew why. Just as the afternoon she'd spent with her family had most likely been the catalyst for the attack, her thoughts now, her reliving of that emotional suffocation she'd felt in her parents' home, were enough to aggravate the situation. She hadn't had an attack in months. The coincidence was too great. And her only recourse was to sit still and force herself to relax until the medication took effect.

It was more easily said than done. The air was cold; already she felt chilled. Her thoughts strayed to possibilities of pneumonia, and she shivered. She had to get up, to move on. Yet it hurt to breathe; she couldn't run yet. Knowing she'd again been brainwashed by her family into accepting her frailty and angered by it in turn, she nonetheless grew frightened. Removing the inhalator, she administered a second half dose, then waited, timing her breathing, forcibly steadying it, closing her eyes and concentrating totally on the good, strong aspects of her life. Her heartbeat came rapidly, forcibly, its drumming a loud reminder of how far she'd come, both literally and figuratively.

She barely heard the footsteps until they were upon her. When they stopped abruptly, she jerked open her eyes and looked up. A large figure of a man loomed over her. In the instant she realized how totally vulnerable she was to another kind of attack. Her pulse faltered, then whipped ahead with the jaggedness of her breath.

"Are . . . are you all right?" the man asked hesitantly, unable to decide whether she'd simply stopped for breath, whether she was crying, or whether she was indeed hurt or ill.

Dana's voice was weak, a breathy "Yes." If the man intended harm, she told herself, he would surely have skipped even that simple question of concern. And he was a runner. She saw now that the wide stripe on his jacket was of the similar reflective material as her own, as were dual stripes down the sides of his legs and the markings on his sneakers. The darkness withheld all else.

"You're not hurt?" His voice was deep, concerned yet gentle.

She simply shook her head as she fought to control her wheezing. Even in the dark, with this runner a total stranger, she had an enormous amount of pride. He shouldn't see her struggle for breath. He should simply assume that she'd overdone her run.

But he saw everything. "You've been running?" She nodded. "Too much?" She nodded again, and he promptly hunkered down before her. "Can't catch your breath?"

"I'll be all right," she gasped softly. "I just need a minute." In truth, she'd already had nearly ten. She felt cold and weak. And the medicine should have begun to work.

The stranger stared at her for a minute longer, noting both her pallor and the labored working of her chest. Then, having made his decision, he stood quickly. "You need help," he announced, tossing a glance at the dark, deserted landscape. "I think it'd be fastest if I just run back for my car." He'd already begun to unzip his jacket. "It's about two miles down the road, but there don't seem to be any other houses nearer. I can be back in fifteen minutes to pick you up."

"I'll be fine," she protested, but he

ignored her to wrap his Windbreaker around her in offer of its slight additional warmth.

"Don't move," he ordered, then was off, leaving her to stare after him in dismay.

That another runner would come to her aid wasn't surprising. In the four years that she'd been pounding the roads, the runners she'd passed had been invariably friendly. There were a small group of regulars, each running singly, some running daily, others two or three times a week. In a unique kind of way they'd become friends. They never talked other than to share a wave or a smile in passing. She didn't know their names, or where they lived or worked. She doubted she'd even recognize them dressed in street clothes. But she shared a bond with them— the same bond that had brought this man to her side moments earlier.

No, it wasn't his stopping that surprised her. It was that he seemed to have silently and calmly analyzed the situation and taken it upon himself to remedy it ... and she had let him! After years of resenting her parents' overblown concern, she was letting a stranger, a fellow runner, no less, do the same.

She was all right. Even now, as she huddled

beneath the folds of the man's large jacket, she felt better. She'd known it would pass. Wasn't so much of it a state of mind? Today, back in the house in which she'd grown up, she was her parents' daughter. As her parents' daughter, she was an asthmatic. And as an asthmatic, she had attacks. It was as simple as that.

Now, though, she was herself. Dana Madison. A woman who, in the last four years, had discovered a whole new world— one of fresh air and exercise and, for the first time in her life, freedom from constant medication.

With a slow, indrawn breath, she smiled her relief. Much better. She took another breath, then stood. Home—her small cottage on a corner of the Gantling estate—was no more than a mile and a half down the road in the opposite direction from that in which the stranger had disappeared. Testing her strength, she bobbed several times. When her knees seemed steady enough, she leaned against a nearby tree, palms flat against its bark, body angled out, to stretch the muscles at the backs of her legs. Inhaling loudly and clearly, she was satisfied.

She broke into a gentle run then, pausing

once to retrace her steps, slipping the stranger's jacket from her shoulders and spreading it atop the rock where its reflective stripe would catch his eye, before heading home. Any lingering weakness she felt took second place to her keen sense of victory. She'd won after all. She'd beaten it again.

High on an aura of power, she easily made it home in the fifteen minutes it would have taken the stranger to get his car and return. Of course, he'd had a head start. He would have already found his jacket and realized that she'd recovered on her own. And she did feel a twinge of guilt at having disturbed his run. But she had tried to protest, she reasoned, as she let herself in and began to strip the sweat-dampened running suit from her body. She'd tried to tell him that she was all right, though even she had only half believed it at the time. Perhaps another day she'd have occasion to thank him.

Having tugged off her wool cap and tossed her light-weight outer suit to a chair, she peeled off her sweat shirt, then her leotards and T-shirt. Naked from the waist up, she sat on the chair to remove her wool socks and footless dancing tights. Clad only in the briefest of nylon briefs, she padded across the bedroom to the bathroom, where she turned on the shower full force and waited for the water to heat. Facing the mirror, she brushed through the long tangle of her hair, its sandy blond length responding immediately to both natural bristle and humidity. Then, with the steam of the shower beginning to seep above the glass enclosure and slowly descending into the room, she lifted the weight of her hair from her neck and stared at herself in the mirror.

Too pale? Too thin? She saw neither. What she did see, in fact, brought an even more complementary blush to her cheeks. Before her stood a woman whose flesh was moist and creamy, whose arms were well-toned, whose breasts were full and high. Turning to the side, she indulged herself a minute longer, pleased at the slimness of her waist, the flatness of her stomach, the tautness of her bottom. Fifteen pounds? Was that all? But then, the fifteen pounds had been only half the story. Running had done it. Running had done just about everything!

With the fogging up of the mirror, she turned, let her hair fall, slipped the nylon briefs over her hips and stepped into the shower.

⌘   ⌘   ⌘

Driving slowly along the route she'd taken, Russ Ettinger scanned the roadway for any sign of a woman in distress, but there was none. He'd come another three miles from where he'd left her, from where he'd found his jacket so carefully placed atop the rock. He doubted she'd have been able to go farther than this unless she was up to doing six-minute miles—a feat that would have been impossible, given the way she'd been breathing.

Eyes straining, he scoured the road again. With nothing but the headlights of his BMW as a guide, he cursed the darkness and the dense landscape which could absorb every bit of light as fully as it could absorb the small figure of a woman in trouble. Turning into a private drive, he reversed direction and combed the trail as he headed back to his sister's house. Nothing. *Could* she be in further trouble? His headlights had failed to catch the slightest sign of a reflective stripe. Surely she wouldn't have crawled into the trees to collapse!

You're letting your imagination run wild,

he told himself, deciding he'd overreacted. She'd been winded; that was all. She'd pushed herself too far, perhaps had over-partied on New Year's Eve or simply under-estimated the cold. Most likely she was home by now and all right. Very probably, a friend had come by and picked her up.

Who was she? He couldn't help but recall her face. It had a fragility about it, different from the more rugged look of the usual runner. It invited protection. The corner of his mouth slanted mischievously; perhaps he ought to run in Sondra's neighborhood more often.

With a one-wristed flick, he guided the car up the drive toward the house, stepping hard on the brake by the side door. Sondra was there to meet him.

"Any luck?" she asked, holding the door open, then following his tall figure back into the kitchen.

He dragged the wool cap from his head to reveal a disheveled headful of sweat-matted brown hair. "No. She got away."

Sondra Grant sent her brother a chiding frown. "I thought this was a rescue mission, not a hunt. You said the woman was hope-lessly winded."

"She was, when I left her." He ran his fingers through his hair, then propped a hand on his hip. "She must have recovered."

"Recovered what?" came a voice from the hall, instantly followed by Sondra's daughter, Danielle, whose attention was riveted on her uncle.

"Not recovered *what*," Sondra scolded softly. "Recovered *from* what. How many times have I told you not to barge headlong into the middle of discussions?"

The teenager was undaunted. "Who recovered from what, Russ?"

"*Uncle* Russ—"

"Mother, Russ doesn't care what I call him."

"Well, *I* do, and he's still your uncle. You owe him that little bit of respect. After all, he does have twenty-three years on you."

Russ shot a wild glance at the ceiling, then eyed his niece. "Pretty soon she'll have you pushing my wheelchair." In truth, he could do without the "uncle," too. He was well used to children far younger than Danielle calling him by his first name; it went with the territory. *That* territory. *This,* though, was Sondra's territory. If he didn't respect her wishes, Danielle never would.

Still, he couldn't restrain the play of amusement at the corner of his lips. "Besides," he said, holding out a long arm under which his niece took instant refuge, "if you call me plain 'Russ,' someone is apt to think we're sweethearts."

"Lovers," Danielle amended, grinning broadly.

"Lovers? No way, metal mouth," Russ countered as he smacked a kiss on her forehead.

His niece blushed then, a refreshingly young response to the gentle banter. "It's just a retainer," she protested. "And besides, I never wear it out. The dentist and Mom are the only ones who say I need it. My teeth are perfectly straight now."

He gave her shoulder a squeeze. "Let's keep 'em that way."

"That's what *I* say," Sondra muttered from behind the refrigerator door, where she'd gone in search of milk for hot chocolate.

Danielle frowned once at her before looking more brightly at her uncle. "So, what was all the excitement about? All I could hear was talk of rescue missions and recoveries."

With a gentle pat on the back, Russ

released her and moved toward the door. "Runner in trouble. False alarm. I'm going to change, Sondra. Be right back."

By the time he'd showered and dressed, the hot chocolate was on the table in the kitchen. Danielle was on the phone in the living room. Sondra was sitting, waiting, deep in thought.

"Don't worry about her," Russ said, taking a seat opposite his sister. "She'll be fine."

"She's impossible, Russ! She takes joy in defying me about everything. If it's not homework, it's that retainer or clothes or allowance or curfew."

"It's the stage," he answered, then paused to take a sip of his drink before continuing on a philosophic vein. "Mothers and daughters have to suffer through it sometimes."

"And how do *you* know so much about it?" Sondra asked half humorously. "What does a confirmed bachelor like you know about mother-daughter relations?"

If she expected a flippant response, he surprised her by replying in earnest. "I see them every day, Sandy. Families are constantly at the slopes. Mothers and teenaged daughters very often seem to have trouble, that's all. It would almost be funny, if it weren't for the fact that both are usually miserable."

"Hmph. Let me tell you about it. For as much of a comfort she can be at times, at others she's an absolute wretch."

Russ gave a crooked smile. "I'm sure she'd say the same about you." He paused to study Sondra's look of utter frustration. "Take it easy. Be patient. She'll be all right."

His sister sighed sadly. "I suppose so. I think it's the second-guessing that's the worst. I assumed she'd gotten over Brian's death, but maybe she hasn't. Maybe she needs a father figure in the house. Maybe *I* should be home with her more. I sometimes feel so guilty working."

"You don't have to work, you know. I'd be happy to give you whatever you need."

"I need to work for *me*. I guess *I* haven't gotten over his death yet. And I'm sure that's why I'm so concerned about Danny. I hate the thought of bad feelings between us. We're all we have. I really do need her."

Russ reached out to squeeze his sister's hand. "It must be lonely for you at times."

Covering his hand, she slowly nodded. "At times like these, especially. The holidays are tough. If it weren't for you . . ." Her voice trailed off and she looked up.

"If it weren't for me you'd probably have

forced yourself to go out and meet people. You really should, you know."

She gave a disinterested shrug. "I will—in time."

"Don't waste it, Sandy. Life is too short."

"Look who's talking. What about you? No wife, no children. What are *you* waiting for?"

He was suddenly sober. "Nothing."

"What do you mean, nothing? You don't want a wife or kids?"

"Maybe not."

"That's absurd, Russ! Look at how wonderful you are to us. You love kids. I can see it in how you deal with Danielle, not to mention the kids who constantly pass through the ski school. And as for women, you could have your pick." When her brother did nothing more than dart her a narrow glance, she went on. "Lord only knows you meet enough. Don't tell me there aren't a few that interest you."

His jaw tensed. "A few . . . for fun here and there."

"But nothing permanent?"

"No."

"Why not?" she prodded him, but her voice was gentle. "I could understand it when you were racing. You were too enthralled with the sport to be truly interested in any-one or anything else. Then when you hurt yourself and had to stop—".

"Sandy, that's enough."

Disagreeing, she barreled on. "I could understand it then. You weren't sure what was going to be financially. But now you've got no excuse. You own half the mountain, for God's sake! So if it's not an issue of money—"

This time Russ's voice was more taut. "Drop it, Sandy."

"But—"

"It's not your affair."

"It is. You're my brother. I worry about you, just as you worry about us."

"He's just sowing his wild oats, Mother."

Both heads flew to the door to see a smug-faced Danielle lounging against its jamb, arms crossed over her chest, looking for all the world as if she'd been standing there forever.

"Danielle!"

"It's true." The teenager straightened and sauntered to the table. "And there's nothing wrong with that." She put a proprietary arm on her uncle's shoulder. "If Uncle Russ wants to play the field, you should let him. It *isn't*

your affair any more than my dating Greg
Florentino is."

"Now, that's where you're wrong, young
lady," Russ broke in. "Who, when, and where
you date *is* your mother's business."

"It shouldn't be," the girl argued, momentarily taken aback by Russ's siding with the
enemy.

"But it is. And the sooner you accept
that, the better. Besides," he grinned, "sowing wild oats is for men. Women need to be
protected."

"A sexist comment if I've ever heard one,"
Sondra ventured before cautioning herself to
mark her words. While she was all for
women's liberation when it came to equal
pay and equal opportunity, when it came to
sexual freedom, specifically that of her own
daughter, she was a tad more conservative.
"Women need to be protected? Or is it men
who have the need to protect?"

Russ opened his mouth to argue, then
shut it on second thought. She could be
right, he mused. Why else would he have
stopped today in the middle of running,
turned around, dashed back home to get his
car and gone in search of a woman he'd
determined needed his help, when in fact

she appeared to have been perfectly capable of helping herself?

"Good question." He frowned, then started in mid-breath. "Are there many joggers around here?"

Both Sondra and Danielle eyed him sharply. "What do joggers have to do with man's need to protect?" Danielle asked.

Russ gave her a playful wink. "I'm changing the subject." Then playfulness yielded to curiosity as he turned his attention to his sister. "*Are* there regular runners on these streets?"

Sondra shrugged. "Like any other town around. Sure."

"Do you know any of them?"

Sondra looked at Danielle in shared bewilderment, then both looked back at Russ. "I suppose," Sondra said. "The fellow down the street runs every so often. And there's a woman a little farther on who comes by." She paused to eye him, askance. "You're wondering about the runner you saw today?"

"Mmmm." He certainly was. Mention of protectiveness had brought her to mind.

Danielle's face lit up. "The rescue mission?"

"It turned out to be no mission at all," Russ admitted sheepishly. "When I got back there with the car, she was gone."

"What did she look like?" Sondra asked.

"I don't know."

Danielle grimaced. "'You don't know'? You're destroying the image, Uncle Russ. I thought ladies' men *always* noticed things like that."

"Not quite, little girl," Russ drawled. "There are times when other things are more important. Such as breathing. The lady was having a hard time breathing. I wasn't about to start guessing her measurements."

With Danielle momentarily chastised though not far off the mark, Sondra regarded her brother indulgently. "What *did* you guess at?"

"Not much. It was pretty dark."

"You must have seen something. Her hair, for instance. What color was it?"

Propping his forearms on the table, Russ buried one fist inside the other. "She wore a wool cap. I couldn't really see. If I had to guess, I'd say she was fair though."

"Now we're getting somewhere," Danielle interjected. "How tall was she?"

"I have no idea. She was sitting on a rock."

"And she didn't stand up to wave you down?"

"No, Danielle." The drawl was back, as was the twist at the corner of his mouth. "Nor did she hike up her skirt to lure me with a black-gartered thigh." When his niece sat back in her chair, deflated once again, he softened. "She was having trouble breathing," he repeated patiently. "I found her sitting on a rock gasping for air. At the time I didn't think she could stand, much less run off somewhere. I must have been wrong. There couldn't have been more than fifteen minutes between the time I left her and the time I returned with the car, and she was gone."

Sondra's gaze held its share of doubt. "How did you know where to look? I mean, as you've said, it was dark. And you're certainly not as familiar with the road here as you are at your place. Maybe you got the wrong rock."

"My jacket was lying there, laid out very neatly where it was sure to catch my eye."

"Your jacket?" This from Danielle, with a spark of renewed interest.

Russ spared her no more than a passing glance. "When I found her, she was cold. I put my jacket over her shoulders."

"That's lovely, Uncle Russ. Chivalry *is* alive and well—"

"That's enough, Danny," her mother scolded, though she barely took her gaze from her brother. There was something in his eyes that fascinated her. "Did you notice *anything* else about her?"

Russ frowned and studied his hands. He recalled that he'd debated lifting her and carrying her home. She was very slim, almost waifish. "She wore a running suit not very different from mine."

"Was it from the shop?" Danielle asked, only to have her enthusiasm dampened by her uncle's glower.

"Even if it had been broad daylight and we'd simply stopped by the side of the road to talk, I couldn't have known that unless I'd asked her. In addition to our label, I stock many of the same name brands that other sports stores carry. You know that."

"Yeah, but *could* it have been yours?"

He shrugged. "I suppose."

"Then there's a chance she's been in the store. She may have bought her gear from you. You may have waited on her yourself. Just think of the romantic possibilities."

Russ looked at Sondra. "You're right.

She's impossible. Isn't there something you can do to shut her up short of soldering her mouth closed?"

"But I'm serious," Danielle protested. "Don't you think it was fate that on New Year's Day you should stumble across her? And how typical of the romantic tragedy that she should vanish before you returned for her?"

"Don't you have some homework to do?" Sondra asked.

"On New Year's Day?"

"Then listen to the radio."

"This is more interesting."

"Call Stacey."

"I tried. She's not back yet."

Russ stood and held out his hands for peace. "Ladies, ladies, this is where I take off."

"Oh, no, Russ," Sondra protested. "Stay awhile longer."

"I'd love to, but I really do have to run."

"You just did," Danielle put in smartly. In response, Russ clapped a hand to her neck and playfully drew her from the chair.

"*You* come with me," he said, then made his way to the living room. When the kitchen door had swung shut behind the two, he put an arm around her shoulders. "Go easy on your mom, okay, Danny?"

"Go easy on *her*? She's hard as nails!"

"She's not, and you know it. It's been tough for her without your dad. She's trying her best. And you know how much she loves you."

"I know. But it's stifling sometimes."

"Maybe to you. You're just itching for everything at once. Slow down. You'll be grown up before you know it." With an affectionate glance at her upturned face, he patted her arm, signaling the end of the lecture. "Listen, how about if I pick you up at school next Friday. I need your help."

"My help? Whatever on?"

"Picking a birthday gift for your mother. I want to get her something special, but I'm no good with sizes and colors. How about it?"

Danielle had been on such shopping trips with her uncle before. Almost invariably she came home with something for herself as well. "Sure, Uncle Russ," she grinned. "That sounds great."

"Good." Russ released her, took his coat from the hall closet, and pulled it on. The knee-length camel coat was well in keeping with the slacks and sweater he wore for the holiday, though far more dressy than his usual jeans, turtleneck, and parka. Bending lithely, he tucked his running gear under his arm, then stood and gave Danielle a peck on the cheek. "Friday. Right after school." Left unsaid was that she wasn't to dally forever at her locker with her friends. She'd done that once and had had to face his wrath. He doubted she'd do it again.

Passing through the kitchen, he hugged Sondra. "Thanks for everything. Dinner was delicious."

His sister pulled herself from deep thought to return his hug. "Thank you for being here. I only hope we didn't run you off," she added on an apologetic note.

"Don't be silly, Sandy. You're family."

"Which means that if we weren't, you'd have left during that little fight about Greg at the dinner table?"

"Which means that I love you and Danielle, boy troubles and all. Danielle will get her act together. She's a bright kid. She knows the guy's a jerk, but the more you speak out against him, the more she'll stand up for him. Keep calm. And give her time."

"Give her time . . . give her time." Sondra smiled and shook her head. "You must have a lot more patience than I do."

"I'm her uncle," he said, eyes twinkling as he crossed the room. "An uncle can have infinite patience, especially since he leaves when the going gets rough. So long, Sandy." He was halfway out the door when his sister's voice stopped him.

"Good luck."

He paused and looked back. "On what?"

"Finding her."

"Finding who?"

"The runner who ran away."

His first impulse was to categorically deny his sister's assumption. Then he stopped himself, pondered her words, and smiled. "It would be a challenge, wouldn't it?"

"Uh-huh."

"Could be interesting . . ."

"Particularly if she's married or engaged or otherwise attached."

"Particularly."

"You wouldn't . . ." Sondra teased him, knowing that as much of a playboy as he'd always been, Russ drew the line there.

"No. That's not my style. But if she were free . . ." There was pure, if exaggerated lechery in his gaze.

"How old was she, anyway?"

"Old enough," he quipped without pause,

but half wondered. She'd struck him as being so small, so vulnerable.

"Then heaven help her." Sondra smiled and waved Russ along, little realizing the potency of the bug she'd put in his ear.

TWO

He'd half begun to feel like the prince with the glass slipper. Cinderella eluded him. Not that he'd ever seen her in a ball gown, much less held her in his arms. But her image stuck with him throughout the week, such that by its end he decided that his niece had very definitely inherited her romanticism from the Ettinger side of the family.

Though the mountain hummed all week with the post holiday skiers, most of the crowd had returned to the city, leaving Ross, as director of the ski school, more time to divide between the slopes and his store in town. Wherever he went, his eye was sharp, subtly scanning the faces before him for hint of a delicate woman, a woman with fine-sculpted features, a fair-haired woman with eyes wide enough to capture him, to hold him prisoner. For that was just what they'd done when he'd found her trying to catch her breath by the side of the road. He couldn't forget those eyes. They'd held fear and vulnerability, and a strange sense of pride. They'd suggested a depth to the woman, a strength within to compensate for any weakness of the body.

He'd been puzzled by her, puzzled by his own reaction to her. And the fact that he couldn't shake her image puzzled him all the more as the week went on.

As promised, he picked Danielle up at school on Friday. As wisely but silently agreed, she was right on time. Where he'd expected her to be first and foremost anxious to get to the stores though, she had something else in mind.

"A favor, Uncle Russ?"

"Sure . . . uh, within limits."

She grinned. "You'll like this one."

"Oh? Then tell me. I'm curious."

"The library. Can we stop at the library first?"

Teasing her, he put a hand to her forehead. "Are you feeling all right?" He'd been under the distinct impression that Danielle Grant was down on school.

She batted his hand away with a lopsided grin. "I'm fine. But I need to pick up some books for a report."

His gaze narrowed in good-natured suspicion. "Okay, who's there?"

"Who's where?"

"At the library."

"No one!"

"Not even Greg?"

Her chuckle was conclusive. "No way."

"Then why the rush on Friday afternoon? Nothing can be due until Monday."

"That's just it. I have this thing that's supposed to be in rough draft form by then. And if I can stop by the library now, I'll have the books at home to work with."

He arched a brow. "You were planning to do work tomorrow?"

"Sunday."

"And tomorrow?" He knew as did she that the library was open all day Saturday.

Caught in the trap, she blushed. "Tomorrow I, uh, I wanted to go to the Game Room." Wall-to-wall electronic games, plus half of the sophomore and junior classes.

Her uncle raised his head knowingly. "That's *the* place now?" Danielle nodded. "Who were you planning to go with?"

"My friends."

"Girl friends?"

"Mostly.

"Plus Greg?" Russ asked, unable to ignore her incriminating blush. When Danielle hesitated, then nodded again, he grew softly serious. "Does your mother know?"

"Oh, yes. She gave me permission. For the afternoon."

"Then you could go to the library in the morning." He was only half teasing, curious to see just how she'd respond.

It was with horror. "On Saturday morning? But I don't get up until ten, and then I have to shower and wash my hair. Come on, Uncle Russ. It will take me only a few minutes."

He looked at her then, drawing out the torment debating the issue. Danielle waited, watching, wondering what objection he could possibly have. Then she caught the gleam in his eye and she scowled. "If you're done playing games, could we get on to the library? After all, the sooner we get there, the sooner we can leave."

Her chiding tone, grown-up yet not, brought an easy chuckle from him. "Saw right through me, did you?"

She looked out the window, but the scowl had softened. "You're a pushover, Uncle Russ. A real softie. Why some woman hasn't snapped you up is beyond me."

"Me too," Russ quipped, starting the engine and pulling away from the curb. He had no intention of getting into that particular discussion with a sixteen-year-old girl just beginning to feel the power of her femininity. The fact that he wasn't any woman's for the snapping would have spawned discussions better avoided. It was bad enough when Sondra started in; Danielle, he didn't need.

The library proved harmless enough at first. While Danielle went to work with the card catalogue, Russ sauntered into the reading room, sought out the newest *Sports Illustrated* from the alphabetically arranged shelves, and settled into a nearby chair to relax. Heavyweight boxing, the subject of the cover story, had never really been his thing though. His mind wandered. When an elderly man who'd been sitting reading the newspaper at a nearby table stood, Russ studied his bent figure as it shuffled toward the door. When, several minutes later, a young woman came in laden with books, he watched her find a place across the room and open a notebook.

Eyes back on the boxing, he turned several more pages, then flipped through to an article on college basketball. It was somewhat better, though still not particularly absorbing. When a pair of slender legs sheathed in burgundy tights entered his line of vision, he was easily distracted. Shapely calves, narrow ankles, a smooth stretch of thin stocking from light gray leather flats to the hem of a softly pleated gray wool skirt—he was fascinated. As his eyes rose, though, she left the rack, magazine in hand, and headed for the main room. Russ had time only to take in a burgundy belt, a soft white blouse, and a neat knot of light hair at her nape, before she rounded the corner and disappeared.

With a sigh he returned to his magazine, but his thoughts were irrevocably averted. Strange, he mused, how one woman could attract a man while another could leave him cold. He shot a glance at the woman buried in the books across the room. She was attractive enough—dark, slim, with long hair that shimmered gently around her shoulders—but he could as easily flip back to heavy-weight boxing. The woman who'd just left, on the other hand, intrigued him. Perhaps it was *because* she'd left, left without giving him a full look to satisfy his typically masculine curiosity. His eye scanned what he could see of the main room, but there was no sign of her.

Flipping the magazine shut in defeat, he laid his head against the back of the chair and closed his eyes, wondering what had come over him that he should be so intrigued by a pair of dark-stockinged legs. It had been too long. That was it. He'd have to give Marcy a call, or perhaps Elaine. But, God, how they bored him! For that matter, his entire social life bored him. Where once he'd thrived on party-going and constant excitement, now he found it tiresome. Was it old age? Did he suddenly see things differently as he stood on the threshold of forty? Most men his age were getting their second winds, living it up as if to prove themselves as young as ever.

Not him. He'd been living it up since his knee had forced him out of racing nearly thirteen years earlier. Thirteen years of women, not a one who inspired the promise of tomorrow. But it hadn't been a totally wasted time. Rather, he'd forged the basis of security, taking the money he'd earned in endorsements and investing it first in the mountain's ski resort development, then in the ski school itself. He'd done well, yet he had no one to indulge but Sondra and Danielle. Did he want it different after all these years? Could he ever settle down and finally accept the fact that game knee or not, he no longer had to prove himself?

Danielle's appearance was well timed to rescue him from the intensity of his thoughts. "All set?" he whispered, dropping his magazine on its shelf as he stood.

Danielle was struggling to juggle four books in one arm as she dug with the other hand into her pocket for her card. Russ quickly relieved her of the books.

"I just have to sign these out," she said.

Side by side, they left the reading room. "Did you get what you wanted?"

"Uh-huh."

He turned the books sideways to read the titles from their spines. "*Women and the Vote? The Suffragette Cause?*" He put on a pained frown. "Your teacher assigned these?"

"Actually, we had half a dozen topics to choose from. I chose this one myself."

They'd arrived at the checkout desk and he set the books down. "That figures," he teased in a whisper. "Women and power. What else is new?"

"Your bias is showing, Uncle Russ," she whispered back smugly, then shot a glance at the librarian, who'd put down the magazine she was reading, to help her. "Older men can be so old-fashioned at times," she blithely informed the woman as she handed her the card.

The librarian smiled at Danielle over the rims of large, pink-tinted glasses. Then she looked down. "Do you know that this card has expired?" she asked the girl.

Unable to imagine better punishment for his niece, whose pert bubble popped instantly, Russ chuckled. When the librarian turned her gaze on him though, his laugh died. Sobering instantly, he swallowed hard. In the periphery were a gray skirt, a burgundy belt, a soft white blouse. More directly within his gaze was a thick sweep of ash blond hair, twisted neatly back from a small, delicately etched face. But it was her eyes, wide through her glasses, that struck the paralyzing inner chord. It was *her*. The runner he'd stopped to help the weekend before. The one who'd gotten away. He was sure of it. Those eyes, clear and comprehensive, held the depth that made her unique.

Strange for a man known to be suave and composed, his heart beat loudly as, before his eyes, the woman calmly turned her attention back to Danielle. She hadn't recognized him. That, too, was strange. But then, it had been dark. And he'd worn different clothes and a hat. Besides, she'd been gasping for breath.

Not so now. She was calm and collected. "If you'd like, I can type up a new one for you," she offered to Danielle in a gentle, easy voice. The stereotypical librarian, minus some thirty years, he mused.

"Could you?" Danielle asked. "I really need these books."

"Sure." Her smile was soft and bright. "You're still living at the same address?"

"Uh-huh."

"Excuse me then. I'll be right back."

Russ watched as she swiveled on her high stool to free herself of the desk. He noted the grace with which she stood, felt another thrill go through him at the sight of the slim, burgundy-covered legs he'd first seen back in the reading room. Athletic? Very possibly. Women runners never did seem to develop the unsightly calf muscles men did. It was a biological thing, as was so much of what he felt at that minute.

At the far end of the desk now, the librarian quickly typed out a new card, then was back. She reached for the books Danielle had chosen, opened them to the pocket on the inside back cover, and, with the help of a machine that recorded with the press of a button both Danielle's card and that of each book, proceeded to sign them out.

Russ didn't take his eyes from her once. He found her looks fascinating—far more fragile than those of the usual runner. But then, he'd had that same thought the night he'd found her. Looking at her now, he felt a similar surge of protectiveness. He conjured the image of her leaving work in the dark, a lone figure struggling forward against the numbing chill of the January wind. His eye dropped to her hand, its bare length adorned by nothing more than the scalloped cuff of her blouse at her wrist. The other hand was the same. But Russ's first thought was not one of relief that she wore neither engagement nor wedding ring; rather his thought was of taking that hand in his and keeping it warm.

"There you go." Smiling again, the librarian turned the books around and slid the stack gently toward Danielle, who whispered her thanks, pocketed her card, lifted the books in her arms and turned to leave.

Russ couldn't. Not quite yet. He cleared his throat. "Uh, excuse me . . ." His brows were drawn together in puzzlement, not so much as to what he felt as to what he should do about it. He'd never approached a librarian before. The only thing he was sure about at the moment was that he should keep his voice low. She was looking at him now, her expression solicitous though blank. From what he could see, she really didn't recognize him. But she was waiting for him to speak, as was a bemused Danielle, who'd stopped several feet away and turned back to stare. He cleared his throat a second time. "Uh, I . . . uh, I think . . ." Then he took a breath and forced out the words on a note of frustration. "Haven't we met somewhere before?"

From behind him, Danielle tittered. But Russ was oblivious to her, concentrating solely on the woman before him, who very slowly shook her head.

"I don't believe so," she stated in a half whisper. "Have you been in before?"

"No. But it wasn't here." Studying her face and the supreme innocence it bore, he wondered if he was wrong. His gaze touched her features one by one, never quite sure again until he reached her eyes. Damn it, it was her! He'd put money on it! "Do you run?"

"Run?" she echoed in surprise.

"I was running on New Year's Day and I saw someone who looked very much like you. You live here in town, don't you?"

Danielle had taken a step closer, but mercifully kept quiet. She'd never seen her uncle in action, and was amazed at his quiet intensity. She'd somehow assumed he'd be cocky, smooth, a true Lothario. Yet he seemed somehow unsure of himself, unless that, too, was part of the act.

"Yes," the librarian replied slowly. "I live in town. But I'm sure you must be mistaken."

"Do you run?" He repeated his question gently.

To Danielle's eye, the librarian wavered for a minute. When she seemed to catch herself, it was to don a veneer of composure. Even her large glasses, though, couldn't hide a lingering disturbance in her gaze.

"Uncle Russ?" Danielle whispered, reacting out of an odd impulse to ease the woman's discomfort. Her uncle looked around, abruptly recalling his niece's presence. "Shouldn't we be going?"

"Uh, sure." Then he turned once more to the woman behind the desk. "Perhaps I was wrong. I'm sorry."

The librarian offered the trace of a smile. "That's perfectly all right," she murmured in a voice just breathy enough to convince Russ that he wasn't wrong at all. But he knew where to find her when he wanted to pursue the issue.

When. Not if. As he nodded his farewell, his eye fell momentarily to the magazine she'd been reading. He was familiar enough with *Runner's World* to recognize the logo in its corner instantly. And then there was her hand, strangely taut on the edge of the desk as she slipped back onto her seat.

Oh, he'd be back, without a doubt. There was that depth to be plumbed. He felt suddenly more enthusiastic about the future than he had in months.

From her perch, Dana watched him leave. She breathed deeply. Her thoughts skipped back to that run she'd taken on New Year's Day. Was this the man who'd been so kind to her? Then she'd suffered from a mild attack of asthma. Her shortness of breath now had an entirely different cause.

Yes, he was tall. Even in her winded state that night, she'd noticed. His good looks— that was something else. Whereas she'd been in no condition to judge his build before, she now easily saw how fit he was. Broad-chested but lean and leggy, she could easily imagine him a runner. There was a hardy air about him, an aura of physical energy tempered by urbanity.

Grant. That was the name she'd typed on the girl's card. His niece. She'd called him Uncle Russ. Was it Russ Grant? Or was this his sister's daughter? Did he live nearby, as his niece did? There was always the chance that his presence on the local road that night had been an extension of a holiday visit. Dana had never seen him before; she would have known if she had. A man with that kind of intensity wasn't one to be forgotten.

Intensity. Single-mindedness. It was a theme that cropped up repeatedly in the running books and magazines she pored through regularly. Eyes still on the door through which he'd passed, she imagined him a world-class runner, even a marathoner. She was well out of his league at any rate.

With a sigh she glanced down at her magazine and absently turned a page. It was just as well she hadn't identified herself as the woman he'd found on the road that night. Then he would have asked—she would have had to explain. And she was tired of explaining. That was one of the things her new life was about. No one looked at her differently. No one knew there was anything wrong. For the first time in her life, she was as capable, as whole, as the next person.

Pride was a powerful thing, she mused. Just as that night she hadn't wanted him to know the true cause of her difficulty, now, having seen him off the road, she felt justified. This Russ whoever-he-was was so obviously at the peak of health that by comparison she paled anyway. Not that he'd made the comparison—not that she'd ever see him again for that matter—but she did have her self-respect. In some ways it was more potent medicine than any a doctor could prescribe.

Out of the corner of her eye she could see the button on the desk phone blinking. Buoyantly, she stretched for the receiver. "Circulation," she answered in that tone, halfway between talk and whisper, she'd dubbed "library low."

"Dana? It's me."

"Liz! Is everything all right?" Liz Mann was her neighbor and dear friend. She rarely called the library. "Bethie's okay, isn't she?" Bethie was Liz's four-year-old daughter. She'd been sick during the early part of the week, though the report the night before had been good.

"Bethie's fine. It's John."

John was Liz's older brother, Dana's sometime date. "He just called to say that he can't get out of Boston for another hour. He probably won't be here until eight. Which kind of shoots the movie."

John was bringing a friend, Liz's sometime date, and the four had planned an evening together. "That's all right," Dana said. "Why don't you all just come to my place? I'd be glad to put something together."

"I offered the same, but John wouldn't hear of it. They want to take us *out* to dinner. He suggested I make reservations at the Spud Farm."

"Mmm. Sounds good! I could go for a good, thick steak."

"Hah! And knowing you, you'll run it off before we go. Anyway, that's why I wanted to call. If you have errands to do after work, don't rush."

Dana smiled into the phone. "Fine." Then the wheels in her mind began to turn. "I think I will stop in at the market. Can I get you anything?"

There was a momentary pause, then a deep, appreciative drawl. "Oh, Dana, it'd be great if you could pick up some coffee and a dozen eggs. That'd save me a trip later."

"Sure. Anything else?"

Again a pause. "I suppose I could use some butter. And if you happen to see any danish that looks fresh . . ."

Reaching for a pencil, Dana chuckled. "Wait a minute. I'd better write this down." She did so. "Coffee, eggs, butter, danish."

"And peanut butter."

"Is that it?"

"That's it."

With the phone balanced between her jaw and shoulder, she tore off the paper, folded it, then tucked it into her purse, which was sitting below the desk. "I'll drop them off on the way home."

"You've got money?"

"Just got paid."

"Great. I'll pay you back when you get here. Thanks, Dana. Bye-bye."

Dana hung up the phone feeling particularly

good. Having spent a lifetime being helped, it pleased her to do the helping for a change. Liz was a loyal friend, newly divorced and with a one-year-old child when she'd moved into a small house adjacent to the estate grounds. She and Dana had hit it off instantly, and the relationship had been far from one-sided. Just as Dana might pick up supplies at the market or simply lend an ear when the other suffered divorce pains, as she had early on, so Liz gave of the warmth of her home and daughter, welcoming Dana, encouraging her, slowly learning the details of Dana's past yet ever pushing her toward the future.

Dana's thoughts were interrupted when a young man approached and slid several books her way. She grinned in instant recognition. "How are you, Jim?"

"Fine, Dana. Too much work though."

"I thought you had the whole month of January off."

"Hah! That's what they say. Independent studies can be more demanding than regular classes though."

She reached for the books and quickly signed them out. "But we're all proud of you. Dean's list for another semester—that's terrific!"

Jim leaned his rangy frame across the desk and gave her an endearing smile. "Yeah, but you still won't go out with me, will you?"

"Nope." She spoke slowly, with good-humored emphasis on each and every word. "I don't rob cradles."

He took barely a breath. "I like those glasses."

"You've seen them before."

"I like them anyway. You look pretty."

"Compliments, compliments. How I love them." She sighed, then dropped her voice an octave. "They'll get you nowhere though."

"You're sure?" he drawled.

"I'm sure."

Inhaling deeply, Jimmy Mitchell stood to his six-foot height, straightened his shoulders, and sighed with mock solemnity. "I suppose this lonely scholar will just have to turn to his books for comfort."

"And Carolyn Wald?"

He frowned so suddenly it was comical. "How did you know about Carolyn Wald?"

Dana gave a pert shrug. "I have my sources."

Jim shook his head. "You're a sharpie, Miss Madison." But he'd say no more. With a wave he was off, leaving the librarian to help a woman who approached, then another, then a man looking for information on wood stoves, and another seeking books on travel in the Caribbean.

It was this aspect of library work, the research end, that Dana loved most—helping people, seeking an occasional elusive newspaper article on microfilm, sharing excitement over a wood stove, an island in the Caribbean, a particular battle of the Civil War, or a novel by an unknown but talented writer. And she enjoyed the people themselves, many of whom she'd come to recognize as they filed in and out of the stacks.

As a child she'd spent hours in the library, one of the few places not considered off limits. It was also one of the few holdovers from her childhood that she hadn't been able to leave when she'd made her bid for independence. Even aside from the fact that her degree had been in library science, hence her job training, she wouldn't have thought to seek something else. She loved it here. The library was, to her, a place to dream of different times and far-off places. It was a peaceful spot, an old stone building with soft lighting, easy chairs, the smell of antiquity, and a window on the world. It was an easy ten-minute drive from her house, a thankful fifty-minute drive from that of her parents. And it wanted her, asthma and all.

Back at the circulation desk, she was kept busy by what seemed a steady stream of townsfolk. Five o'clock came quickly upon her. She took several minutes to gather together the books she wanted to bring home for the weekend, then retrieved her coat and headed for the door. Struck on its threshold, she stopped. Did she have time? She eyed her watch calculatingly. There was the bank, then the supermarket, plus a stop at Liz's before a hot bath at home. With John delayed and dinner late, she might well make it.

A slow smile spread across her lips as she backtracked to the circulation desk, pulled a telephone book from the lower drawer, flipped through the pages until she'd arrived at the proper one, then reached for the phone and dialed.

A deep voice answered promptly. "Good Sport."

Dana took a breath. "Uh, yes. Can you tell me how late you'll be open today?"

"Eight o'clock, ma'am."

She grinned. "Great! Thanks!"

Eagerly anticipating a new pair of running

shoes for her morning run, she sped toward the bank and the supermarket, dashing into Liz's house with one bundle, into her own with the other, pausing only long enough to store the perishables in the refrigerator before hurrying back to the car and heading in the opposite direction from town.

Good Sport was two towns over, a thirty-minute drive but well worth the trip. It was the finest sporting-equipment store for miles. In it, Dana was like a child in a candy store, exposed to all kinds of goodies that had always been denied her. Passing the racks of skis and boots, of goggles and parkas and bib overalls, skirting the tennis rackets and designer shorts and tops, the climbing gear and fishing poles, she sought out the corner that was most special, most attainable.

Running gear was very simple. Shorts and singlets. Rain suits, hats, lightweight gloves. And books. She spent as long as she dared with the latter, choosing a thick, newly released volume on women and running before turning to the point of her visit, the sneakers. She knew what she wanted. Her eye fell on it instantly. The Mercedes of running shoes. Her New Year's gift to herself.

"Would you like some help?" The voice that roused her from her fascination was that of a good-looking blond-haired man whose ruddy tan Nordic sweater and slim-fitting jeans suggested he'd come directly from the ski slopes.

"Yes," she smiled more shyly. It was still a new experience for her to see herself in this world. One part of her would always feel like an interloper. "I'd like to try a pair of these. Size seven. As narrow as they come."

She half expected to be turned down, to have the handsome face chide her with a statement the likes of Are you sure you're allowed to have these? Instead, he smiled knowingly. "You've done your research. There aren't that many that do come in narrow widths. This is one." He motioned to a nearby chair. "Why don't you have a seat. I'll be with you in a minute." And he disappeared through the nearby doorway that led to the stock room.

Too filled with energy to sit quite yet, Dana wandered around the running corner, fingering the fine nylon shorts she'd buy come spring, setting her eye on its matching singlet. When the man returned, she quickly took the seat he'd suggested and watched as he opened the box. The sneakers were pale blue with a white stripe on either side in the marking unique to the manufacturer. Slipping them on her feet, she felt positively naughty . . . and ecstatic. She indulged her helper as he poked at the toes and the sides, checking for the fit before finally allowing her to stand.

"They feel terrific!"

Her breathy exclamation floated into the back room, bringing a dark head up from its focus on the account books. Neither Dana nor the salesman were aware of the attention suddenly given their conversation.

"They should," the salesman remarked gently. "The fit is good. And the shoe itself can't be beat."

She walked around for several delighted moments before sitting down once more. "I'll take them," she declared, infinitely satisfied.

As the man tugged at the laces to remove the shoes, he looked up at her, fully serious. "You're not planning to run the MTC ten-miler in these, are you?"

It was the highest compliment he could have paid her. The Maine Track Club's race was fast approaching. That he thought she might compete brought a blush of pleasure to her cheeks. "No. I wasn't planning to. Why?"

"As fine as these are, they're like any other running shoe in that they'll give you terrible blisters over the distance unless they are properly broken in. And there's not much time left for that."

"Aah. I see. But, no, I'll break them in gently." She grinned sheepishly. "I've got a few older pairs that I can wear in between."

The man cocked a tawny brow. "Only a few? Myself, I don't run. But I'm told that a runner can never part with old running shoes. True?"

Dana couldn't help but laugh. "That's funny. I thought it was only me. I have four pairs in that closet. Then I'm not crazy?" she asked whimsically, standing to walk with the man to the register.

In the back room the dark head turned toward the door. Its owner stood very slowly and moved to its opening. Propping one hand above his head on the doorjamb and another on his hip, he stared in the direction of the cash register.

Dana paid for the book and the sneakers, chatting quietly with the salesman all the while. It was only when the transaction was finished and the blond-haired man came from behind the counter that Dana's eye caught the tall, dark form in the background. Her heart beat faster. She momentarily lost her train of thought. What was he doing here? In the back room? And, clear as day, he saw her. He recognized her. He knew.

THREE

Dana mustered every ounce of her reserve to face the salesman again, thank him with a quiet smile, and leave with a semblance of poise.

Russ didn't move. He simply stared after her until she disappeared into the night. Only then did he come forward.

"Who was she, Buddy?"

"That woman?" He shot a glance toward the darkness, then shrugged. "A new customer. A runner."

"Do you know her?"

He shook his head. "Never seen her before. Not that I'd mind seeing her again. She wasn't bad looking."

"Did you get her name?"

Buddy Verdunn looked at his boss closely

then. "No. She paid in cash. When I asked if she wanted to be put on our mailing list, she said she was on it already. I guess she has been in here before. Must have been one of the others who waited on her though. I'd remember."

"I'm sure you would," Russ observed wryly, seeing a younger version of himself in the self-assured ski bum. Though Buddy hadn't won the races Russ had, he had good looks and youth. Russ found himself bothered at the thought of this fair-haired Romeo going after his nameless runner. She wasn't one to be used and discarded, but treasured.

Turning on his heel, he retraced his steps to the backroom desk and his books. Having dropped Danielle home at five, he'd hoped to accomplish something here. But his mind wandered, coming back time and again to focus on her face. *Her* face. He'd known it had been her the instant he'd heard her voice. Why hadn't he just come out to talk with her instead of waiting until she'd had one foot out the door? Oh, she'd seen him all right. He'd felt the full force of her eyes when she'd looked back and encountered his gaze. And now she knew that he knew that she'd been the one on the road that night. So where did he go from here?

Dana had no such question in mind as, stunned, she climbed into her car and headed back home. It was simply a matter of disappearing into the night and hoping never to see this man again. He frightened her. He touched her. He reached her in odd ways, at odd times. She felt totally outclassed.

Monday afternoon, though, when she looked up from the card file she was sorting, into the dark and exceedingly virile image that had haunted her against her will through much of the weekend, she sensed that this was one man from whom she'd be unable to run. He had her cornered, caught on her own turf. There was nothing for her to do but to face him.

"Uh, hello," she murmured, forcing a smile. "Is there something I can do for you?"

He stood still for a while, entranced by her face, strangely stunned to see her, though he'd been planning this visit since Saturday. He'd stopped in then and found it to be her day off. Now, though, she was here, and he didn't know quite where to begin.

He cleared his throat and wondered how eyes could possibly look so blue through pink-tinted lenses. "Yes. You could . . . help me."

She sat at her desk expectantly, looking up, aware once again of his height, of the silent strength he exuded, tongue-tied and all. It was only the latter that gave her courage. "Are you looking for something?"

"You could say that," he said, responding with a dry mouth and a total lack of cockiness to the wide-open question. To go on, though, was something else. He cleared his throat again. "I wanted to get information on ... on coffeemakers." It was the first thing to pop into his mind, and was as good as anything else. "I've got to get a new one. Aren't there ratings somewhere? *Consumer Reports,* that kind of thing?"

His voice was deep, smooth, rubbing her just the right way. Hating her own vulnerability, Dana took a minute to catch her breath. "Yes. That's right. *Consumer Reports.* There are several other publications, too. The most recent issues are over there." She pointed to a nearby table, a shelf above which held the material in question.

Russ glanced in the direction she pointed. "There?" It had been years since he'd used a library this way. "Under coffeemakers," he murmured distractedly.

"That's right."

He nodded his understanding, but didn't move. Nor did Dana. The air between them sizzled with so much more than talk of consumer guides and coffeemakers, that she struggled not to squirm. It was almost a relief when he spoke.

"Do you always get such dumb requests?"

She smiled in relief at his helpless expression. Contrary to her imaginings, he seemed totally unpretentious. "Oh, it's not dumb. And yes, I get similar requests often."

"They don't bore you?"

"Should they? It's my job to help people find what they want." Prompted by some unknown force, she stood. "Come. I'll show you." Within minutes, she had a magazine opened to a comparison of coffeemakers on the current market. "There. Now you can read it. It looks like this one"—she popped a slender forefinger against the model featured prominently—"is the one to buy." She paused to look up. "It's a great way to pick up information."

"If you're into coffeemakers . . ."

Her gaze fell to his lips and the air began to percolate. "That's right," she murmured less confidently. He seemed infinitely close at that minute. Close, and dynamic, and frighteningly intense. She straightened and took a step back. "I'll leave you to read," she murmured, then turned and left before Russ could think of anything warm or witty to say.

Back at the reference desk, she pushed around the cards before her as if they had the power to tell her what it was about this man that struck her so. She realized she'd been sheltered; at times like this she realized how very much. The men she'd known had been gentle and easy-going, and, for the most part, eminently boring. Russ whoever-he-was was different. But then, Alex Kraft had been different too. *That* had been a disaster!

Unable to stifle a shudder, she put two fingers to her temple and lowered her head. It had been months since she'd thought of Alex, and she resented doing so now. Her life was quiet, yet pleasing in its own private way. For the moment she needed nothing else.

"Are you all right?" Russ's voice came to her then in echo of a cold, dark night.

Her head shot up, her eyes flashing in annoyance. But before she was able to utter a sound, his expression of concern blanked out her protest. Then, as she watched, his concern eased, his features relaxed, and a slow smile stole across his lips. "Ah-hah! So there's a bit of fire deep down there after all."

For lack of something better to do, Dana straightened her forefinger against her lips.

His grin only broadened. "Hit the truth, did I?" he asked, assuming her gesture to be one pleading secrecy.

But she shook her head. "You're talking too loudly."

"Oh." His grin faded, though his lips remained relaxed. "What's your name?"

"Dana Madison."

"Have you worked here long?"

"Six years."

"Six years? I thought that librarians nowadays had all kinds of sophisticated degrees."

Her lips twitched helplessly. "We do."

"Come on. You can't be more than twenty-five. Where did you find the time—"

"I'm nearly thirty," she whispered, casting an eye toward a woman at a nearby table. It was an apt reminder of their setting. When Russ spoke again, it was in perfect library low.

"Nearly thirty," he teased gently. "Whew,

that's quite a blow. But it does make things easier."

Dana felt her pulse begin to race. "Things?" she echoed, her eyes widening. She had no way of knowing of the lost-doe look on her face, or of the effect it was having on Russ.

He thrust one hand into the pocket of his slacks, feeling suddenly unsure again. She seemed so delicate, so fragile. He had to tread carefully. "Yes. Well, uh, I wondered if I might . . . if you might join me for . . . coffee, or something."

It was the tentative nature of his approach that enabled her to face him. "Coffee?" she murmured softly. "You've got that on the mind, haven't you?" At first he didn't follow. Reading his puzzled look, she prompted him. "The coffeemaker?"

He tipped his head up in understanding. "The coffeemaker!" Then he gave an endearing smile. "I guess I am a little single-minded." His eyes spoke of far more than coffee though. "How about it? Coffee?"

She shook her head, the perfect excuse at hand. "I can't, I'm working."

"You have to take a break."

"Not for a while. I just had lunch."

"Then I'll wait."

She took a deep breath and looked down. "I'd ... rather you didn't. I don't take much time off, no more than five minutes in the lounge."

"Can I join you there?"

"It's restricted to library personnel."

"Then later? After work. How about a drink?"

"I don't drink."

"Dinner. Surely you eat."

She eyed him defiantly, angry to be prodded so. "Regularly," she said.

He sighed then, and spoke slowly. "But not alone. Is that it? There's someone in your life? I mean, you're not wearing any rings, and I naturally thought—"

"There's no one," she stated quietly.

Russ watched her closely then, trying to decide whether she was shy or frightened or simply turned off. "Is it something I've done?" he asked with such soft pleading that she couldn't help but smile.

"Of course not. It's me. I lead a very ... quiet life." And this man was unsettling. She knew not to play with fire. "I like it that way."

His voice was low but direct. "Is that why you run? To free yourself of the energy you build up leading that quiet life you claim to like?"

For as ill-equipped as she felt in handling men such as this one, Dana was no fool. She knew criticism when she heard it, and she wasn't about to let it go unanswered. "You know nothing about me *or* the life I lead. And as for my reasons for running, they're *mine*." She paused for a breath, then narrowed her gaze on him. "What are you grinning at?"

"You. That flash of fire in your eyes, the flush on your cheeks when you're angry. It's like"—he raised his eyes skyward, searching for the words—"it's like . . . you're a split personality. Here in the library"—he lowered his voice to add the aside—"when no one is harassing you as I am, you're quiet, controlled, and docile. I half suspect, though, that there's a whole other side."

"A wild side?" she asked, amused in spite of herself.

"Not wild." He studied her, tipping his head to the side. "Never wild. Perhaps determined. Headstrong. Defiant." He raised both brows. "Am I warm?"

"Warm," she conceded, all too aware that he'd very nicely gotten around her flare of anger.

"And how am I to get hot if I can't get to know you better?"

At the double entendre, Dana sucked in her breath. "You're not. Warm is all you get. Sorry."

He leaned closer then, his long torso easily bridging the desk. His face was within inches; his breath fanned her cheek. "You're not sorry," he whispered. "You're being determined. Headstrong. Defiant. Which tells me, at least, that I'm getting somewhere. If I'd been unable to penetrate the librarian in you, then I would have been worried."

Dana could barely think, much less speak. She felt mesmerized, caught in the spell of this exceedingly masculine man. His words stirred that very defiance of which he spoke, yet his nearness put it all to shame. She felt torn every which way, angered by her inability to protect herself from his silent invasion of her senses, drawn all the closer with every minute he remained by her side. She was aware of the rush of blood through her veins and knew that he had to hear its pulsing thunder. And she was helpless, helpless to calm it, as helpless against it as she'd once thought herself to be against her own physical condition. But she hadn't been helpless then. And, gritting her teeth, she vowed she wouldn't be helpless now.

With a deep breath she sat back and stared boldly into the dark brown eyes above her. "You'll have to excuse me, but I've got work to do."

The eyes didn't blink. "Russ Ettinger."

"Excuse me?"

"My name is Russell Ettinger." He said each word clearly, soft but distinct. The ghost of a smile hovered around his lips. "I thought you'd like to know, so that you can call me by name next time we see each other. I mean, since I know yours."

"Next time?"

Straightening, he tucked both hands into his pockets and shrugged. "You never know when I'll be in again." He made a broad sweep of the room with eyes that held their share of humor. "This is a pleasant place. I'm surprised I didn't discover it sooner."

Dana pertly tipped up her chin. "So. Do you know which one to buy?"

"Which what?"

"Coffeemaker. Isn't that what you came looking for?"

The ensuing silence, brief but pregnant with meaning, was fitting counterpoint to the gleam in Russ's eye. When, quite instinctively, she began to bristle, the gleam grew gentle, hypnotic in its way.

"Not really," he answered softly. "But then, you knew that, didn't you?"

As he stared at her that last moment, she also knew that he didn't expect an answer. His gaze said as much and more. She knew that he would try to see her again, that this was a man not to be daunted by a one-time refusal. No, she knew that he would be every bit as determined, as headstrong, as defiant as she, and then some. And it frightened her.

"See ya," he called softly as he turned and left.

It was a long time before she was able to concentrate on her work.

"Russ Ettinger?" Liz Mann frowned as she searched her memory for the clue on its outer edge. "Where have I heard that name before? Ettinger . . . Ettinger . . . damn!"

Dana gave Bethie a hug before setting her down with a pat on the bottom. "Don't worry, Liz. If you can't remember, it couldn't be important."

"The name sounds so familiar," she complained. Pushing her hands into long mitts, she opened the oven door and extracted the chicken-and-vegetable casserole she'd made for dinner. "It'll nag at me for the rest of the day." She straightened, casserole in hand. "What does he look like?"

Dana paced her words. "He's tall. Tall and dark."

"And handsome?"

"I suppose," she agreed as indifferently as possible, thinking she'd sounded convincing enough, until Liz caught her on it.

"What do you mean, you 'suppose'?" Liz grinned, carefully placing the casserole on the counter and tugging off the mitts. "Come on, Dana Madison. This is the first time since I've known you that you've come home with a man on the brain. Was he handsome?"

"Yes!" Dana barked begrudgingly.

"And you liked him?"

"No! He was infuriating."

Liz reached for a handful of silverware, then took the tall stool beside Dana's and absently set it out. "In what way infuriating?"

For a minute Dana struggled to put her thoughts into perspective. It seemed an awesome task. "I don't know," she finally murmured. "I guess . . . I guess it was his persistence. He asked me out for coffee and when I refused, he kept pushing."

"Whyever did you refuse?"

"Because I didn't want to go."

"But why not? You had to take a break sometime. Why not for coffee with Russ Ettinger?"

Dana shot her a wry glance. "I didn't even know his name at that point. At least, not his last one." Honesty had bid her tack on the qualification, one she regretted the instant it hit the air. As she'd known would happen, Liz's curiosity was all the more roused.

"But you knew his first?"

"Uh-huh. He was in last Friday with his niece."

"Ah-hah! The plot thickens. So he came in last Friday, saw you at the desk, and made a special trip back on Monday to see you? That's charming, Dana."

"It's not charming. It's downright annoying. I *work* there. I can't spend my time jabbering with some hunk of a man, runner or no."

"Runner?" Liz's tone dropped an octave. "Okay, Dana, give."

Disgusted at herself for her transparency,

Dana hesitated. It took her no more than a minute, though, to realize that if she'd been transparent, it was for a reason. Perhaps she wanted to discuss her feelings after all. They were new and strange. She wanted Liz's support.

Liz was not about to give it. "You're crazy!" she promptly announced at the conclusion of Dana's story. "Crazy and stubborn. The man is obviously interested. What harm could come of seeing him?"

"I know nothing about him, Liz, other than that he has a teenaged niece and something or other to do with a sports shop two towns away."

"Sports shop . . . sports shop . . ." Liz tapped her lip. "Ettinger. Why does that sound so familiar?"

Dana ignored her to rush on. "From the looks of him, he's probably a superb athlete. What could we possibly have in common?"

"You run. That's a start."

"Hah! I run the way millions of other American run, my simple three or four, maybe five miles a day. If he runs, you can bet he does it competitively."

Liz frowned, grasping in vain at random wisps of memory. "So do you, in your way—

run competitively. It's you against a weakness that kept you an invalid for years. Most people would stand in absolute awe of what you've done. Don't put it down."

Dana sighed. "I'm not putting it down, Liz. I'm proud of what I've done. It's meant the world to me. But my running has to be slightly different from Russ's."

Swiveling back to the counter, Liz took some dishes from the cabinet and proceeded to set the table as she spoke. "You'll never know that unless you get to know him. Now, will you?"

It was a point Dana hated to acknowledge. She recalled how she'd felt under a kind of spell at times in his presence, and *that* had been at the library. It terrified her to think what might happen on less safe ground.

"What are you afraid of?" Liz's voice came more softly. Her hand covered Dana's. "Is it involvement that scares you?" When Dana didn't answer, she prodded gently. "You know, I've never asked you this. But I've wanted to. I've known you for three years now, and in that time you've never once expressed more than a passing interest in a man."

"You know how fond I am of John—"

"'Fond' doesn't do it, babe. And forget John. He's my brother. I adore him, but I doubt he's right for you. You need someone who's not only warm and sensitive and caring, but who loves you enough to know when to let go. John's the smothering type. I know that. If he lived any closer, you would have dumped him long ago, and I'd have cheered you on. For God's sake, you haven't come all this way simply to fall into the kind of relationship you've been fighting to escape."

"John's a sweetheart."

"Sweetheart or no, he's wrong for you. But we're getting away from my question. What is it, Dana? What is it that scares you away from involvement?"

There was pain in Dana's eyes as she returned her friend's gaze. "I'm an asthmatic, Liz. I can't escape that fact."

"You've been doing a damn good job of it lately," Liz replied. "And why not? You're perfectly able to control your attacks. For all appearances, you're no different from anyone else."

"But I am. There are still so many things I want to do but can't."

"Like?"

"Like racing. There's a kind of fever that sets in when you run. And all it takes is one reading of a magazine, or one visit to a running store—"

"Like Good Sport?"

"Yes. The fellow who helped me asked if I was planning to run the Track Club's ten-miler. I wish I could. It would be a whole other dimension to running, a whole other dimension to *me*."

"Then why don't you?" Liz asked with such utter calm that Dana was taken aback.

"I have *asthma,* Liz! I can't just go out and run races—"

"Five years ago you were told not to run at all. You didn't listen then, and look at you. You're in better health and far happier than you ever were." She leaned forward. "Listen, I'm certainly no authority on the matter. But if it's something you want to do, why not look into it? There must be someone in the medical field who could give you encouragement."

"My allergist—"

"Your allergist's an ass! He's been against your running all along, hasn't he?"

"Yes."

"Then find someone else. I mean, it's really

a farce, this doctor worship. The field of medicine is no different from any other. If you ask the same question of any five doctors, you're apt to get five different opinions."

Dana smiled. "Your bias is showing."

"Because of Ron?" Liz scowled at the mention of her ex-husband. "He was an ass anyway." She lowered her voice, remembering the little girl in the next room. "Aside from what I might have thought of him as a doctor." She took a breath. "But really, Dana, if racing's what you want, you ought to consider it, just like if a man's what you want . . ." Her voice trailed off on the train of a thought. "Your doctor didn't, uh, he didn't scare you off that, too, did he?"

"Off men?"

"Off sex." There was no point pussyfooting around. Liz had long suspected that Dana might fear physical involvement. It seemed a natural extension of the fear that had been instilled in her from early childhood. It also seemed a dreadful waste.

For the first time, Dana grew noticeably uncomfortable. "We, uh, we never discussed it all that much. I just assumed that . . . that it was all right."

"Does it worry you?"

Dana opened her mouth to offer a hasty no, then closed it with the denial unspoken. In truth, the act of lovemaking terrified her. She doubted she could ever attempt it again.

"I suppose it does worry me." She looked down at her hands as she gave the tempered confession. "There's always that possibility that the . . . the excitement, or whatever, could bring on an attack." When she looked back up, her eyes bore raw pain. "Can you imagine how horrible that'd be?"

Stunned by her friend's fear, the evident extent of which she couldn't begin to imagine, Liz wavered. But it seemed unfair to her that a woman as capable of love as Dana should be denied that richness. "I'm sure it would be awful," she sympathized in the softest of tones, "if it were to happen. But there's no proof that it would." When Dana suddenly bit her lip, Liz ignored the gesture. "You've told me yourself how closely asthma attacks correlate with the state of mind. Look what happens when you run. You *will* yourself to breathe freely. Don't you see? It would be that way with the right man. He would know about your condition and both its cause and your fears. He wouldn't let you have an attack any more than you'd let yourself have one. And in the process"—she broke into a beseeching smile—"you'd let yourself in for something very, very beautiful."

Dana wiped an unbidden tear from the corner of her eye. "Coming from a divorced lady, that's quite a statement."

Reaching to the acrylic napkin holder in the center of the table, Liz picked out three. "My marriage to Ron fell apart for reasons unrelated to sex, Dana. We were always great in bed together. I couldn't deny that any more than I could deny the precious little thing we produced." Her gaze wandered toward the living room door, through which wafted the faint sounds of the television, then grew more distant. "Would you deny yourself that, too?"

It was a question to which Dana had given more thought than many a woman of child-bearing age. It wasn't simply a matter of having a child. There was the matter of health to consider.

As if reading her mind, Liz ventured, "There's many an asthmatic who's given birth. You could survive it easily."

"I could survive it?" Dana asked. "That's not the issue at all. The issue is whether I'd

90

be condemning a helpless child to the hell I spent twenty-five years in living. If a child of mine was asthmatic, I'm not sure I could stand the guilt."

Much as Liz wanted to be supportive, she found herself pulling back. Of all the things she'd imagined hearing from Dana, this wasn't one. Stunned, she slowly shook her head. "You surprise me, Dana. I mean, I'd assumed that you'd be worried about having a child. It'd be only normal. But to feel such self-pity—"

"It's not—"

"It is!" She stood up and turned toward the door. "Dinner, Bethie!" she called, then lowered her voice and faced Dana again. "In the first place, there are medical advances being made every day. If a child of yours were asthmatic—and I do mean *if*—it would have that much more of an advantage than you had. Not that it would be a given that you'd have an asthmatic child. You could have five perfectly healthy children! And besides, even *if* one of those children did suffer from the disease, don't you think that, what with your own background, you'd take a very different attitude toward it than your parents did?" She scowled at the door.

"Bethie! Come on!" Then she took a breath and renewed her attack. "If it's your guilt you're worried about, perhaps you're right. It would be better for you to remain alone all your life. Then the only one afflicted is yourself!"

The appearance of the child cut short her tirade and, as though a curtain had fallen on the issue, the conversation took a lighter turn. Ever in the wings, though, were Liz's words. Neither woman could quite forget they'd been said.

When Dana left shortly after dinner, it was with stilted words of thanks.

"Listen, Dana, I didn't mean—"

"You did, Liz, and don't apologize. For all I know, you may have a point. If nothing else, you've given me something to think about."

And she went home to the cottage she loved so, to the stillness, the aloneness, the freedom to come and go as she wished, the utter absence of anyone to nag her, the denial of anything in the least bit threatening.

She ran. Over the next week, she ran as though there were no tomorrow—harder, faster, longer than she'd ever run before. It was as though, in anger, she dared her asthma to act up, as though she actively defied the fates that had shaped her life so narrowly.

Over and over again as she ran, she pondered Liz's accusation. Was it self-pity that had taken hold? Or was it raw fear? Liz had no way of knowing of the agony of her experience with Alex, of the humiliation she'd felt when, naked in a man's arms for the very first time, she'd begun to gasp for air. Liz could have no comprehension of the raw disgust she'd seen on her would-be lover's face the moment before he'd hauled himself off her and left the room. No, Liz couldn't know. She couldn't possibly know.

But *was* it self-pity she felt? More importantly, on the issue of children, was she taking the easy way out, rationalizing for the sake of the discomfort she felt at the thought of being with a man? What Liz had said was true. It was certainly *not* a given that a child she bore would be asthmatic. Further, what Liz had said about her having learned from her own experience was right. If she had a child similarly afflicted, she would treat it so very differently from the way her parents had treated her that there would be no comparison whatsoever.

What was it then that nagged at her? There seemed to be a catch somewhere, a password that eluded her much as had Liz's identification of the name Russ Ettinger. Russ Ettinger, was he indeed the cause of this soul-searching she'd begun? She wondered who he really was, where he'd come from, where he was headed, and why he'd set his sights on her.

As the week passed, she wondered if she'd see him again. He'd implied as much when he'd given her his name. Russell Ettinger. It was a strong name, had a healthy sound. After a while it had a familiar ring even to her, most definitely because she'd said it so very many times to herself as the days passed.

Time and again in the library she sensed a figure before her desk, only to look up and find it to be one less tall, less virile, less commanding than his. In each instance she breathed a tiny sigh of relief. In each instance, though, that sigh was followed by a vague and unwelcome emptiness.

Each morning she ran, wondering whether he was doing the same and if, by chance, they'd pass each other.

Each evening he ran, wondering the very

same thing. He chose the same hour, the same road on which he'd seen her that very first day. When day after day there was no sign of her, he ventured to try different routes, always coming back to the first in discouragement.

His sister thought he'd gone mad. "Why don't you just go back to the library and ask her out?"

"I asked her for coffee and she wouldn't come. I don't want to make a complete pest of myself."

"Is it at all possible that she's just not interested?"

"I know she is. It's got to be something else."

"And how do you know she is?"

"A man can tell things like that."

"Oh? How?"

"Her cheeks, for one thing. She kept blushing."

"Maybe you embarrassed her. What else?"

"Her eyes. They flickered."

"And they don't flicker for anyone else?"

"How the hell would I know? I know only that there was interest in them. I'm sure of it."

"Brother, you do have a case."

He'd begun to suspect it himself when, rather than subject himself to Sandy's chiding, he took to driving the forty minutes from his place at the end of the day, parking his car half a mile from her house, and running the route from there. Though he caught sight of other runners, many of whom he'd begun to recognize and greet with a wave or an easy word, there was no sign of Dana.

By Friday he was clearly disappointed. By Sunday he was outright discouraged. By the following Wednesday he was more than ready to throw in the towel and visit the library again. It was, ironically, Sandy herself who thwarted those plans.

"Russ?" She called him on the phone early Wednesday morning. "I've got a huge favor to ask."

"Shoot."

"I've got this opportunity to go to a meeting in Boston. It'd be great experience, but I'd have to be gone overnight. I wonder if . . . do you think you'd mind . . . could you . . ."

"Stay at your house? Why not! Danielle's good for a fun dinner. What time does she get home from school?"

Sandy hemmed and hawed then. "Uh,

that's part of the problem, Russ. Today is her hell day."

"Hell day?"

"Yeah. After school she's got to be driven to a three o'clock orthodontist appointment, then she's got a basketball game to cheer at four thirty. That's over near Naples, so it'd be silly for you to drive back and forth. I'd made an appointment for her to have her hair cut at seven, then she's *got* to get home to do homework." She paused to catch her breath. "It's awful of me to even ask this of you—"

"Don't think twice, Sandy. It's all right." Actually, he needed the diversion.

"You'd be able to leave the ski school by two?" she asked timidly.

"Sure." He grinned crookedly. "After all, as you so aptly put it not long ago, I do own half the mountain. That gives me the right to come and go as I please."

"But the school—"

"The school runs so well they won't even notice I'm missing. It's not as if I myself teach."

If there was a bitter edge to his voice, Sandy was too grateful to notice. "Russell, you are an angel! I'll tell my boss I can make it, then go home and get an overnight case. Should I call the school and have them get a message to Danny?"

"No need. I'll be there when classes break. She'll be looking for you anyway. She can't miss me."

Sandy chuckled. "That's for sure. Hey, thanks, Russ. I'll owe you."

"I'll remember that," he threatened, then hung up the phone.

By the time he returned to the house with Danielle that night, it was after eight. The orthodontist had taken longer than was expected. They'd had to race back to the house for Danielle to change before driving all the way to the game, where Russ had no choice but to sit in the stands cheering for a cheerleader while the others cheered the team. Dinner had been wolfed down at a small burger place that had been Danielle's choice. And the hairdresser had kept her waiting for half an hour.

He was exhausted. "Is it always like this?"

Danielle looked calmly up from her books. "Only on Wednesdays. And it's not usually as bad. I see the orthodontist only once a month. And the only reason I had my hair cut today was because Dino didn't have another opening for a week. I was lucky. Mom called in just after someone else cancelled."

Russ shook his head. "Lucky? Your poor mother. And she still manages to juggle that job?" As for himself, he was asleep long before Danielle. His only solace was in waking up that much earlier than usual, in time to take a long run before he'd even be missed.

It was a typically brisk January morning, the kind on which dawn sparkled crisply on the road, the lawn, the trees, and the hills beyond. Wearing his shorts and a sweat shirt, a running suit over them, socks, sneakers, a wool cap, and gloves, he limbered up and set out, applying himself full force, taking advantage of the early morning hour and his own freshness. The eastern sky, dark when he'd left the house, slowly grew more pale in anticipation of the day.

It was a peaceful time. Russ found himself wondering why he didn't run more often at this hour. But, of course, he'd always been a night owl and, as such, depended on these early hours for sleep. Lately he'd run faithfully at dusk in hopes of seeing one Dana Madison. A lot of good that had done him.

Pushing himself harder in punishment for his folly, he tried to decide whether she was worth it. A quiet, bespectacled librarian, who just happened to run? It amazed him to think of the time and energy he'd invested in her on pure impulse. She'd even turned him down once; he had to be crazy! Now he was set to return to the library for another stab? A masochist, no less!

He was vaguely aware of the ache in his knee, but its discomfort was secondary to his need for exertion. He ran harder, wondering who she really was, where she'd come from, where she was headed, why she nagged at him so.

Not far from the three-mile point where he would have turned around, a sharp, familiar pain shot upward from his knee, settling in a violent muscle spasm in his thigh. Catching his breath, he stumbled to the side of the road, where he sank down upon the frozen grass and clutched his leg until the worst of the pain began to ease.

"Damn!" he swore beneath his breath. "Fine time . . ." But no time was ever fine for this kind of thing. In his misery he cursed the fateful day he'd ever taken to skis.

So loudly was the pulse throbbing in his

head that he didn't hear the rhythmic pattern of footsteps until they came to an abrupt halt before him.

There was a pause, then a tentative voice, little more than a breathy whisper. "Russ?"

When he looked up, his patience snapped.

FOUR

What in hell are *you* doing here?" he growled, his eyes dark and dangerous.

Though startled by his vehemence, Dana was eminently aware of his pain. His features, always rich and ruddy in the past, bore a frightening pallor.

"You're hurt?" she asked, kneeling beside him.

"It's not the first time . . . and it won't be the last, damn it!"

"Your knee?"

"Yes, it's my knee. And it's your fault! I've been running all over creation trying to accidentally bump into you. What in the devil are you doing running at *this* hour?"

"I always run at this hour."

"Not on New Year's Day, you didn't."

It took her a minute to recall that day and the events leading up to her impromptu late-afternoon run. "I'd spent the day with my family and was upset." She grimaced at the way he was massaging his thigh. "Is there anything I can do? What is it? A cramp?"

"Among other things," he grumbled, then exploded in renewed outburst. "Damn it! I've been on these roads at that same time every blessed day since, and you mean to tell me that you weren't even running?"

"Not then," she ventured. "I'm sorry you had to waste all that time."

He sliced her an accusatory glance. "It wasn't wasted. Exercise is never wasted. I ran harder than I have in months. I'm sure that's what this"—he nodded toward his knee—"is about."

"Then I'm doubly sorry." She looked up and around. There was neither a house nor a car in sight. "Look, you'll get chilled sitting here like this. Can you walk?"

"Not for a while."

"Your knee has kicked out like this before?" How much it reminded her of her own condition, she mused.

"Many times."

"Then why do you punish it so?"

When his eyes narrowed on her, Dana was, for the first time, reminded that this was the man who so unsettled her. "Because," he growled, "I was foolish enough to want to see you on the road. I thought that if we met by chance, you'd accept it more than my showing up at your library. As it was, you shot me down for coffee. I thought it would be particularly clever if I could pull it off this way."

No longer directed at her, his anger had clearly turned inward, expressed in open self-mockery. How could she fight him? Had he continued to rail at her, she might have lashed out in self-defense. Now that he blamed himself for the plans that had gone awry, though, she couldn't muster an ounce of resentment. Nor could she yet deal with the motivation behind his purported chase—his single-minded wish to see her again. That she simply ignored.

"So, what do you do—about your knee, I mean? Does it just go away by itself? Do you take out your walkie-talkie and call for help? Do we flag down the nearest car?" Not a one had gone by yet. "Or do I run back and get mine?"

He tipped his head to the side. "You'd do that?"

"Of course I would. I'm not a heartless monster. Besides"—she hesitated for a split second, then went on more tentatively—"it's no more than you did for me that night."

"And you ran off. Where did you run to?"

"Home."

"And you were able to?" He frowned in puzzlement. "I can't imagine how. You sounded terrible."

"Just winded," she answered quickly. "It passed." When he eyed her doubtfully, she took a breath. "Anyway, that's past. The question is what to do about you." His hands were busy kneading his thigh. "I thought it was your knee?"

"It was at first." His gaze grew more sharp. He was sure she'd have to remember. It was what he always found so humiliating, the fact that, having been a kind of cult hero, a local superstar for years, he should now be prone to such disablement. "I injured my knee years ago. Whenever I overwork it, it in turn puts added strain on the muscles of my thigh. As soon as the cramp eases, I should be able to limp on it."

Accepting his story with a dubious expression, Dana looked off toward the horizon. "How far have you run?"

"Nearly three miles."

"Three? You can't hobble back three miles! It'd take forever!"

"Damn!" Russ muttered, shoving back his sleeve to get at his watch. "I haven't got forever, and here I sit like a lame old—*aaaaach!*" His words died with a yelp as he tried to lever himself up, then fell back in pain. "Damn! I've got to get back. She'll be worried out of her mind!"

"She?" Without quite realizing it, Dana recoiled. She'd simply assumed he was single, unattached. Why else would he have pursued her this way?

"My niece, Danielle," he explained, sufficiently preoccupied with his leg to be unaware of Dana's reaction. "My sister had to spend the night in Boston, so I offered to stay at their house."

"She's . . . divorced?"

"A widow."

Dana caught in her breath. "I'm sorry." In the instant, she wondered what it would be like to have it all, then lose it. Her eyes widened in sympathy. "That must be very hard on her."

Her gaze, as Russ's met it, was a potent anesthetic. It removed him from the pain of the moment, drawing him in, fascinating him as it had done from the very first. Once more he was struck by a depth in her. She was inherently different from any other woman he'd known, with a capacity for caring, a kind of solemn wisdom whose source evoked his curiosity.

"It is," he murmured more softly, aching to reach out and touch her cheek, to comfort her for his own sister's grief. Then he cleared his throat. "But she handles it well. She's very strong."

As their eyes held for a lingering moment, Dana felt her insides tingle. She felt transparent, vulnerable, as if he could see inside her, could reach something deep within that no other man had ever touched.

Neither was aware of the small sports car until it whizzed by. Shocked, Dana stood and waved frantically at its fast-disappearing taillights. But it was gone in a flash.

"I'll run back and get my car," she announced, turning briefly back toward Russ. "It's only a mile or so down the road." She hesitated. "You won't leave, will you?"

"And pull a Dana Madison? If only I could!" His gaze was mildly punishing. "Anyway, if I were to try, you'd catch up in a minute. When I hobble, I hobble."

She gave him an unsteady smile. "Don't move," she said, holding up her hand to reinforce the command. Then without another word she set off, finding her pace, pushing it as much as she dared. It was a six-minute mile, the first she'd ever done, but she was oblivious to the time as she dashed into her house, grabbed her keys, and set back onto the road in her car.

She half expected that he'd be gone. It would have been poetic justice. She shuddered at the thought of how history repeated itself, at the way the tables had been so easily turned. And now she was in her car driving in search of Russ Ettinger, driving in search of him after having spent the better part of the last two weeks determined to avoid him at all costs. Though she wasn't quite sure what had come over her, she suspected it related to the fact that suddenly, grounded by a bad knee, Russ Ettinger was human. He had a weakness just as she did. He endured, in many ways, her own frustration.

Approaching the spot where she thought she'd left him, she slowed and, heart pounding, scanned the roadside. He'd done it, she moaned silently. He wasn't there. He'd paid her back in kind.

111

Then she took the next curve and went limp with relief. Ahead, his dark form broke the monotony of the roadside, just where she'd left him, his head on his knees. She caught her breath for an instant, overwhelmed with an emotion she couldn't fathom. Then she pulled up beside him and ran around the car.

"How is it?" she asked, dropping to her knees.

His eyes were tired, though relief was written in the abrupt relaxation of his brows, the faint curve of his lips. "Sore. But it will be for a while. Here"—he shifted his weight to his good knee—"give me a hand."

Dana scrambled to her feet and helped him up, wrapping her arm around his waist and taking his weight without complaint. He was lean and strong, his body that much taller and harder than hers. Much as she tried to concentrate solely on getting him to the car, she was abundantly aware of his nearness, of his arm about her shoulder and his side pressed to hers.

"Wait." She gave a breathy gasp as she reached for the handle of the door. Balancing on one foot, Russ put a hand on the roof, waited until the door was open, then managed to ease himself around and into the car with a minimum of discomfort. Dana raced to the driver's side and shifted into gear. "Where to?"

"Just drive straight. I'll direct."

She drove straight. He directed.

"Is it very uncomfortable?" she asked, casting a glance at the hand that continued to rub his thigh.

"It'll do. You're not wearing your glasses." She hadn't been wearing them that other night on the road either.

"I'm farsighted. I wear them only for reading."

"They're pretty."

"Thanks. What do you do at Good Sport?"

"Anything. Everything."

She shot a sidelong glance his way. "Tell me you own it."

"I own it."

"Seriously?"

"Uh-huh. Bear left at the fork. You like the store?"

"Oh, yes! There's so much to see there! I feel . . ." She caught herself, reluctant to tell him that she felt her most rebellious in his store, or why. "I feel as though I could browse there for hours."

113

"You could. I mean, it's all right with me. Do you ski?" She shook her head. "Play tennis?"

"No. I run. That's all."

"That's enough. You do it every day?"

"Uh-huh."

"In snow?" They'd had their share this winter, though recent rains had cleared the lower elevations of their cover.

"As long as the road is clear. Ice frightens me. When I can't feel the pavement, I slow down to a walk."

"Smart. Take your next right."

"How about you? Do you ski? I'm told the snow's great up at—" Sensing Russ's sudden alertness, she caught herself. "Hey, I'm sorry. I suppose you can't, with that knee."

"I do sometimes," was his cautious response. He was beginning to believe that she might not have recognized his name after all. "It's much like running. As long as I don't overdo it, I'm fine. Take a left here. It's the third driveway on the right."

Nodding, she fell silent, pulling moments later onto the gravel drive abutting his sister's house. With a flick of her wrist she turned off the ignition, then quickly rounded the car to help Russ out. Danielle, dressed already, was at the kitchen door to greet them.

"Uncle Russ! What happened?" she cried, looking from Russ to his bent knee to Dana, back at Russ for a split-second before doing a double-take on Dana. She was about to say something when her uncle's warning glance stilled her tongue.

"My knee gave out. Dana was good enough to give me a lift. Dana Madison, my niece, Danielle Grant. Perhaps you remember each other from the library?"

Both remembered well, though Danielle was clearly stunned. The librarian she'd seen had worn a skirt and blouse, large pink glasses, and her hair in a twist. This woman wore a running suit, sneakers, and a wool cap, from the cuff of which her blond hair threatened to spill momentarily. So it was her uncle's mysterious runner after all, she mused. Had it not been for the obvious pain Russ was in, she might have suspected he'd planned the whole thing.

Standing back to hold the door wide, she smiled weakly. "Hi, Dana. Come on in." Then she turned in concern to her uncle. "How did you do it, Uncle Russ?"

He cast her a look of self-disgust, unwilling

to detail the story again. "Suffice it to say that I pushed a little too hard," he grumbled. With Dana's help he managed to cross the room to the table and lower himself into a chair. "Listen, Danny, could you run up to my room and get the Ace bandage that's in my running bag? If I can wrap this knee, it's a start." Danielle was off instantly.

"What else can you do for it?" Dana asked, feeling suddenly helpless. "Does ice help?"

"Sometimes." Setting his hat and gloves on the table, he unzipped his jacket and pulled it off, then reached for the snap of his pants.

Dana felt her mouth go dry. She didn't budge from where she stood rooted before the kitchen counter, and could only watch with innocent fascination as he proceeded to undress. His sweat shirt, bearing the faded logo of the very company that had produced her new running shoes, clung damply to his broad chest. Her eyes widened when the snaps of his lightweight pants gave way and he struggled once more to his feet. Then his arm came out in search of her and, to her amazement, she jumped instantly forward to lend her support. One-handed, he pushed the pants over his lean hips to his thighs, then dropped back into his chair. Without pausing to analyze her actions, Dana knelt before him and eased the pants past his knees, over his sneakers, and off.

When her eye followed the path of his hand to his knee, she sucked in her breath and looked up at him, stunned.

"Pretty ugly, isn't it?" His lips thinned into a wry grimace.

"My God," she whispered, "whatever happened?" His knee bore a network of scars that spoke of an agony of pain. She raised her hand to touch it, then held her hand hovering above his.

"I tore it up—skiing. The scars are momentos of the operations that were supposed to put it back together again." He gave a bitter grunt. "But like Humpty Dumpty—"

"Here, Russ," Danielle bounded back, a large wad of stretch bandage in her hand. "Do you want me to do it?"

"Thanks, honey," he smiled gently, "but I can take care of that. You'd better get some breakfast or you'll be late."

When he began to carefully wrap the bandage around his knee, Dana stood hesitantly. "Does she need a lift? I could drive her on my way."

With a smile of thanks Danielle took a carton of juice from the refrigerator and reached for a doughnut from the box on the counter. "No, no. The bus picks me up at the corner. You'd do me a favor to stay here with him," she cocked her head Russ's way, "until he's sure he can get around."

"I've really got to run—" Dana began, only to be soundly interrupted by Russ.

"Stay! The least I can do to repay you for the rescue is to give you breakfast."

A knowing chuckled came from Danielle. "You should see the breakfasts he gives." She reached for the box of doughnuts. "Want one?"

Feeling more awkward by the minute, Dana rubbed her palms together. "No, thanks. I do have to leave. I feel really grungy. If I don't get back to shower and dress, I'll be late for work."

"It's only seven fifteen," Russ reminded her pointedly.

"And I've got to be at work by nine." She inched toward the door and cast timid glances first at Russ, then at Danielle. "Good seeing you again. So long." With a meek smile she turned and left, hurrying into the cold, slipping quickly into her car, reaching for the key. The key. It was gone. Leaning forward, looking first at the ignition switch, then at the floor in the chance that the key had fallen, she frowned. She stuck her hand beneath the seat and groped blindly, then transferred her search to the sides of the bucket seat. Mystified, she sat back.

Meanwhile in the kitchen Danielle eyed her uncle as if he were daft. "You blew it, Uncle Russ! If she wouldn't stay for breakfast, you could have asked her out for dinner. I mean, here you had her in your own house— in our house—and you just let her go?"

Russ spared no more than a moment's pause from the wrapping of his knee to give a smug smile, which perplexed his niece all the more. "She'll be back."

"She'll be back? How can you be so—" With the firm knock at the back door, she stopped mid-sentence. What she saw through the slice of parted curtain made her glance back at Russ as she answered it.

Dana stood on the other side, smiling kindly at Danielle before tipping her chin up toward Russ. "My keys?" she prompted, holding out a hand in invitation.

It took Danielle no longer to understand. With her faith in her uncle fully restored, she cleared her throat, darted toward the chair on which her coat and books lay, grabbed them up, and squeezed past Dana. "I've got to run. Bye-bye."

"Got lunch money?" Russ called after her disappearing figure.

"Yup," she yelled from the drive. "Hope your knee's better!" And she was gone, leaving Dana to face Russ head-on.

For several seconds she stood and stared expectantly at him, the same hand extended palm up, the other propped atop her hip. Then she wiggled her fingers. "Okay, where are they?"

"In my pocket." Having secured the bandage with two metal clips, he sat back in his chair, infinitely satisfied.

When he made no move to get them for her, Dana crossed to the table, reached for the running pants she'd helped him discard earlier, and fished in the zippered pocket . . . only to find it empty.

"*What* pocket?" she asked less steadily, then watched with growing apprehension as he pointed to the waistband of his running shorts. Like hers, the only pocket was a hidden one, concealed for convenience's sake on the inside. "Could I have them?"

He shook his head. "Not until after breakfast."

"Russ, I can't stay! I'll be late enough as it is."

Untouched by her plea, he simply smiled. "You've got nearly an hour and a half. Just for today you can skip the newspaper in favor of a few minutes with me."

How he knew that she habitually spent those twenty minutes reading the paper over breakfast each morning, she couldn't imagine. But he seemed to have the knack—for this morning at least—of being one step ahead of her. And disturbed as she was, she was also realistic. If the price of her keys was breakfast, she had little choice.

"You play a mean game," she commented, plopping herself into a chair.

"When it's the only one I can win . . ." he began, then let his words trail off as he turned his eye to the refrigerator. "So, what'll it be?" He took a deep breath and maneuvered himself out of his chair. When he winced once, Dana bolted forward. But his outspread hand held her at bay. "It's all right," he gritted out. "The movement will do it good."

"Do you really believe that?" she asked with a dubious eye. "I'd think the best thing for it would be rest."

"If I gave in to every twinge, I'd be an invalid of the first order." His voice was hard and he tugged the refrigerator door open with unnecessary force. "I don't think I could bear that!"

Dana stared, hearing his words and the vehemence with which they were spoken, knowing exactly what he was saying, for she'd been down that road herself all too often. Strange, she mused, to find these feelings in a man she'd assumed to be the supreme athlete. It made him all the more appealing.

"Okay, we've got eggs and toast." He leaned lower. "I think she's got some bacon in here somewhere."

"I don't really eat much breakfast. A doughnut will do fine."

Turning his head, he gave her the once over. "You could do with more. Running wears off a hell of a lot of calories."

"What would you eat?"

He paused then, straightened, and closed the refrigerator door more quietly. "I'm not much of a cook or a morning person, as if you couldn't guess."

"You were out early enough today."

He scowled, but the expression lacked

harshness. "That was a fluke. I'm not terribly experienced at being a parent. By the time I got back here with Danielle last night after driving her from one thing to the next, I was dead. I think it's been years since I was in bed at ten."

"You haven't any children of your own?"

"I never married. You'll have coffee, won't you?" When she nodded, he set to work with the coffeemaker.

"Do you live far from here?"

"On the other side of the mountain."

"Near the store?"

"Not far."

"Is that where you spend most of your time?"

Measuring out the proper amount of water, he deftly poured it into the machine. "Some. I'm the director of the ski school at West Ridge."

"Really?" she exclaimed, then glanced down at his knee and flinched. "You *are* bucking it, aren't you?" she murmured, only half to herself but in total admiration of his grit.

"Hmmm?"

She shook her head. Not only did she not want to repeat the thought, but her eye lingered on the strength of his leg above and below the bandage, on his other leg, an unbroken expanse of firm-sinewed flesh. "You've been away?" she asked on impulse.

"Away?"

"Your legs. They look tanned." Tanned and well-formed, hair-rough, utterly masculine.

"I spent the week before Christmas on St. Thomas. The islands are beautiful."

"They are," she breathed, then tore her gaze from his legs, praying that he hadn't read her mind.

"You've been there?" he asked, reaching for a pair of mugs.

"Uh, no, not exactly. But I've read about them many times. There are always people coming into the library looking for travel information."

He studied her more intently. "So you dream."

"Yes." Her voice was light and airy, made tremulous by the power of his gaze. "I'll get there someday."

With a sigh he filled the mugs. "Cream and sugar?"

"Black. Here, let me do something—"

"There's nothing to do." But he reached

for the box of doughnuts and held it out. "You can take this." The box was followed by two plates. Then, limping to the refrigerator, he extracted a pint of cream and added a dollop to his own coffee.

"Is it any better, the knee?" she asked as she watched him move unevenly around.

"It's getting there."

"Why don't you sit down?"

"I will." He made it to the table with the two cups in hand, put them down, then followed suit. She couldn't help but notice the tautness of his jaw.

"Are you sure you should be up and around?"

"Damn it, I'm all right!" he thundered, his eyes as dark as the most ominous of storm clouds. "I'm not a helpless fool, at least not helpless, though I must be a fool for having run after you the way I did. Serves me right," he muttered to himself, taking a death grip on his coffee cup before narrowing his gaze. "But I've survived for years with this blasted knee, and I'm sure I'll make it for several more . . . *without* your pity."

Dana winced, then struggled to swallow the thick lump in her throat. "It's not pity I feel," she ventured quietly. "It's just that it's

hard to watch another human being in pain."
For, more so than even the physical, she saw
his emotional torment. And she cared. Much
as she couldn't admit it to him, for some
unfathomable reason she did care. Perhaps it
was the fact that she understood his anger,
that she felt an affinity born of like circumstance. She didn't know. She didn't stop to
ponder it. But she cared. That much she did
know.

He must have seen something in her
gaze, for he seemed suddenly to catch himself and grow calmer. "Hey, listen, I'm sorry.
That was wrong of me."

His tone was gentle enough to do the
trick. With a quick toss of her head, she
looked down. "It's all right," she said softly.
"You needed to blow off steam."

"Do you ever?"

"Explode?" She smiled shyly. "Actually,
now that I think of it, I don't really. I'm a very
placid soul. But I run. That helps."

"And what's your frustration about?" he
asked so softly that she felt the tingle begin
again, lurking somewhere in the heart of her,
somewhere unexpected and unexplored.

She took a gulp of her coffee and nearly
burned her mouth, managing but barely to

hide the momentary discomfort. "Frustration?" she gasped, then steadied her voice. "Uh, the usual things, I guess. I think about the past and the future and wonder whether I'm missing all kinds of things that I'll come to regret one day."

"And are you?" he asked, pushing the doughnut box her way.

"I don't know. I'm still wondering." She reached inside for one honey-dipped and rolled in coconut. "Mmmm. Someone's got good taste."

"Me," he announced quite without conscience. "I just knew you'd be coming for breakfast."

"You're full of it."

"Not yet." With a lopsided grin he helped himself to a plump jelly doughnut. "What about your parents?" He took a big bite, managing by some miracle to divide the jelly between his mouth and the doughnut without dripping a drop.

"My parents?"

"Before—when you found me earlier—you said that you'd been running late on New Year's Day because you were upset. They live nearby?"

"Near enough," she said with an edge.

"And you don't get along?"

"Oh, we do! It's just that . . . well, we don't always see eye to eye on things. There's one part of them—make that the major part—that will always see me as their helpless little girl."

"Still? But you're nearly thirty"—he held up a hand and lowered his voice—"your admission verbatim."

Not knowing her medical history, he couldn't possibly understand. And since she wasn't about to enlighten him, she had to go easy on her parents. "Their hearts are in the right place. I suppose it must be hard to let go."

"You live alone, don't you?"

"Yes."

"Then it's understandable that they'd worry."

"Do yours?" she shot back indignantly. "I mean, you live alone, don't you? Or do you?"

The abrupt switch of her expression from defiant to dismayed brought a grin to his lips. "I do."

Relief brought instant recovery. "And do your parents worry?"

"My parents are dead," he said quietly, then rushed on when he saw her cringe, "but if they weren't, I think they'd do fine. It's different for a man."

"Is it?" she asked, subdued yet determined to make her point. "Why should it be any different? I mean, it's not as though we're living in a city with millions of people crushed in on top of one another and crime and violence rampant. The backwoods of Maine aren't exactly a concrete jungle."

"No," he conceded, trying to reconcile the protectiveness she evoked in him with a more objective reasoning. "But there is an age-old tradition of women being thought of as the weaker sex. As inapt as it might be, your parents are of the generation that hasn't quite adapted. I'm not condoning it, mind you, just trying to understand."

The problem, she realized, was that he couldn't fully understand the situation unless he knew the whole truth. It was safer to simply steer the conversation elsewhere.

"Well," she sighed, turning the coffee cup in her hands, "it's all right, at any rate. My parents and I get along just fine from a distance. And they're really pretty good about leaving me alone. Holidays can't be avoided." As she talked, Russ had grown more serious. When she fell silent, she realized that he was looking at her hard. "Is . . . is something wrong?"

He continued to stare, an exquisite depth to his gaze. "Do you believe in fate?"

"Excuse me?"

"Fate. Do you believe in it?"

"I don't know."

"I do. It was fated, you know, our meeting. That first night on the road, then twice more by accident. Someone up there wants to get us together."

She forced a shallow laugh. "It was coincidence. That's all."

"Don't believe it for a minute," he returned, his eyes deep and mellow. "Coincidence doesn't happen like that, over and over again. I mean, here we are in my sister's kitchen, like two kids who are being shown the hard way that they have more in common than they think."

"You've got my keys. That's why we're here."

There was only a hint of amusement in his gaze. "But why did I take those keys? Who put the bug in my ear?"

It wasn't the bug in his ear that worried her. It was the supreme gentleness of his expression, the haunting lilt of his voice, a sound that shimmered through her with growing awareness of something else far more dangerous that they might share.

"Some little devil," she breathed unsteadily. "And you mean to tell me that my fate is in *his* hands?" She shook her head and, swallowing hard, stood to escape with her cup to the sink. It was an ill-advised move. Russ was behind her with a speed that defied the sorry state of his knee.

"I mean to tell you that your fate is in *my* hands," he murmured ever so softly by her ear, "that our fates are intertwined, that my fate is every bit as much in your hands as the reverse." When he paused for a breath, Dana held hers, unable to move, much less breathe. "There's reason why we're here, reason why neither of us has ever married—"

"I never said—"

"But you haven't been married, have you?"

She wondered how he'd known and feared that he had to have sensed a certain naivete in her. Though she had many male friends, she'd never had a lover in the truest of senses. "No, but—"

"There's a reason, Dana."

She shook her head and whispered a tremulous "I've got to leave." But his hands were on her shoulders and his large body hemmed her in as very slowly he turned her to face him. "Please, I have to go," she begged breathlessly, her eyes round and soulfully blue.

"You haven't got your keys," he murmured, his face mere inches from hers.

"May I . . . may I have them?"

"You can get them." He limped back a step. Neither of them noticed the falter in his gait. "You know where they are," he whispered, releasing her shoulders and letting his arms fall to his sides.

Dana felt the flush on her cheeks as though it burned her from the inside out. "They're in your pocket. Please?" When he simply shook his head, she sensed that burning sensation begin to sizzle slowly down her neck. Every inch of her body was aware of him. He stood tall, his shoulders dwarfing her, his torso tapering to the waist and hips and thighs that broadcast "Man!" from every pore.

To get her keys meant to touch him. Her palms felt suddenly as damp as her lips felt dry. While she could relieve the latter with the moisture of her tongue, the former seemed a hopeless cause against the windbreaking fabric of her running suit.

She had no choice. She needed the keys.

The thought of what might happen if she lingered was more terrifying by far than the thought of simply touching Russ. Simply touching Russ? As she inched her hand toward the waistband of his shorts, she realized that there was nothing simple in such a touch. It was frightening, exhilarating, terrifying.

Her fingertips made contact with the elastic band, its soft nylon covering far less threatening than anything else she could see. A man's body was so different, so taut and firm, with bulges rather than curves. And, to her untrained eye at least, Russell Ettinger was certainly well-endowed. His running shorts concealed little. She bit her lip to keep from making a sound.

Her heart pounding with embarrassing clarity, she slid her fingers beneath his waistband and fumbled blindly for the pocket on the inside of his shorts. She could feel the keys, knew they were there. She could also feel the taut, constricting muscles of his abdomen. For the life of her though, she couldn't find the flap that would allow her access to the pocket. When Russ's hand clamped down over hers to instantly still its movement, her head shot up in alarm.

"What frightens you, Dana?" he asked softly. His eyes bore repetition of the question as they touched each of her features in turn. "Every time I look at you I sense it."

FIVE

Dana swallowed and, unable to answer, simply shook her head. What could she say? That much as she craved it at this moment, a man's touch terrified her? For she did crave it, more so than she ever had in her life. She was drawn to Russ, had been all along. But, yes, it terrified her, terrified her to think of the intimacy, the expectancy that might ensue.

His gentle smile held a hint of puzzlement. "I could never hurt you. You know that, don't you?"

"No," she managed to protest in a whisper. "I hardly know you. How could I possibly know that?"

His hands came up to frame her face, lightly, tenderly. "Because there's something about you that makes me go all soft inside. Hell," he chuckled softly, "I can't even blame you for my bum knee without feeling guilty as sin." Then his smile faded. "There's something about you that makes me want to take you in my arms and protect you from every possible danger in the world."

"But if you're the danger . . . ?" She said it without thinking, direct from mind to tongue.

"I'm not, Dana. Where is the harm in wanting to be with someone, to give to someone, to love someone? There's nothing but good in that."

"But I'm not there," she cried breathlessly. "Don't you see, it's not good if it puts demands on me that I just can't meet."

"Come on." He eyed her, askance. "You can meet any demand I make and then some." His hands framed her face, his thumbs moving in caress of her cheeks, tracing light, hypnotic circles of slow seduction. "I can see it in your eyes, Dana," he went on in a deep, smooth voice. "There's a loneliness there—a loneliness identical to mine."

"I'm not lonely!" she gasped.

"Then . . . alone."

"If I'm alone much of the time, it's by choice." That, at least was the truth.

"But choices are always changing. Perhaps you've had no alternative until now." He shook his head in wonder. "Your eyes tell so much."

His voice shimmered in the air, its sound enveloping her in a deep velvet haze from which she had to struggle to escape. "It's your imagination," she cried, growing frantic. "You see what you want to see, rather than what's there. You don't know me at all, Russ!" She caught in her breath, then rasped, "This is madness!"

"It is." His gaze adored her lips, kissing them without a touch. "A very lovely one."

If it was a spell he wove, Dana was fast becoming ensnared. She shook her head slowly from side to side in a last attempt to break free. "Insanity, Russ. There's so much you don't know!"

Russ knew only that he saw the same familiar fear in her eyes and that more than anything, he wanted to free her from it. For there was passion beneath; he saw it lurking in her depths. She was right. There was so much he didn't know. But there was time. And at the moment he couldn't imagine anything more important than the fact of her in his arms, the tremor of her body so close to his, the lingering grip of her hand branding the mark of her fingers on his stomach.

The slow shake of her head, as though a reminder, drew his attention to the top of her head. Then, feeling as though he were unwrapping a long-awaited gift on Christmas morning, he gently tugged at her wool cap until it came free in his hand, letting spill the luxuriant length of ash blond hair he'd only been able to imagine before. The gift pleased and excited him as no other ever had.

"Russ . . . I have to . . . leave." Her voice seemed to come a long distance and with great effort. She couldn't think with his fingers combing through her hair and his eyes dark and direct. Her own fingers? She grew suddenly aware that while one gripped the edge of the counter behind, the other clung desperately to the waistband of his shorts, seeming glued to him, reveling in his warmth, his solidity. Mustering remnants of sanity, she wrenched it away as she might a recalcitrant child from the rim of a steaming caldron.

"Your hair is beautiful," he whispered.

"It's sweaty and messy. I've got to get home—"

"Warm and damp isn't sweaty and messy.

It's seductive. I've never seen it down like this." Entranced, he stroked its soft, silken length from crown to shoulder, drawing it forward, following its graceful cascade farther. When the back of his hand accidentally brushed the tip of her breast, she gasped.

Her own sensitivity shocked her. It wasn't disgust she felt, or shyness, but rather a burgeoning arousal.

Russ instantly read her fear in the large blue eyes he found so transparent. "It's all right, Dana," he breathed as he buried his hands in the golden mass on either side of her face. "It's all right."

Dana knew what was coming. She craved it; she dreaded it. It excited her; it terrified her. Locked in an inner war of emotional extremes, she tried to pull away, if for no other purpose than to buy the time to reconcile her battling senses. But his grip only tightened, firm without hurting, and he held her face tilted up as his own lowered slowly, inevitably.

His lips feather-brushed hers in tentative exploration, his breath mingling intimately with hers. Again and again he repeated the caress, inching around her mouth with a gentleness that sensitized every point. She wanted to pull back but couldn't. The grip of his hands eased, yet she was held by a far more potent force. He lured her with his warmth, demanding nothing that she wasn't ready to give.

She fought a losing battle. For, if he thought he'd received a gift, the one he gave her was every bit as irresistible. She'd been kissed before and on more than one occasion, yet never with the kind of reverence with which Russ kissed her now. His ease, his lack of demand, were the very force that bound her in place, the very lure that most effectively crushed her defenses. Momentarily robbed of all thought to resist, she could only breathe deep of him, of his scent that was new, raw, shockingly heady, and ultimately male, as primal as the response her deepest instincts craved to give.

Sensing her tentative acquiescence, the sleek filly calmed by soft words and gentle strokings, he sought further conquest in the warm, moist kisses he pressed to her cheeks, her eyes, her brows. Eyes closed, she was helpless to defend herself, too mesmerized by the exquisite pleasure created by his touch to think of anything but its continuation.

Her body felt suddenly alive and vibrant, more attuned to life than ever before. Minute by minute her cravings grew, blinding her to all but the heat in her veins, to all but the source of the heat, this vital man whose hands now wreaked havoc on the slender curve of her shoulders. Powerless to contemplate past or future, she knew only the present. It was, in its odd way, familiar—a more sublime version of the high of running, the second wind, then the one within that that bore the euphoria that overrode pain and fatigue to make it all worthwhile. As with running, she had to keep on. She felt too good to stop.

Her lips parted with a soft sigh of nascent desire. As if it were the signal he'd awaited, Russ captured her lips in a kiss rich and full, a kiss she desperately needed. His mouth moved over hers in its firm way, tasting and caressing, responding to her response with an ever-broadening embrace. One hand slid to the back of her neck in support, the other slipped beneath her arm and molded to her waist, drawing her from the counter, in turn molding her to his silently clamoring frame.

It was all he could do to contain his

drive. His limbs trembled with the effort. Forgotten was the knee that threatened collapse. Dana's lithe body provided all the strength it lacked and more. She was perfect for him, as he'd known she'd be, slender and pliant, fitting him as if they'd emerged from companion casts. And they had. He was surer of it by the minute. Never a particularly religious man, he was nonetheless convinced that they were indeed meant for each other. She felt so right in his arms, so very right. Not once before in his life had he ever thought this about a woman.

Quite unknowingly, Dana's thoughts ran along a parallel vein. She'd never even remotely experienced anything as exhilarating, as delightfully breathtaking. Never before had she known anything akin to the wild ache that ran riot through her body and settled in a knot deep in her belly. Was it a tingling? A burning? A throbbing? A sweet, sweet pain? She didn't know. But it pointed to a dimension of herself she'd never known existed, one she couldn't help but explore.

Driven by instinct, she opened her mouth beneath his lips, as eager to sample the firm texture of him as to offer invitation for a deepening of the kiss. Her invitation was accepted instantly. Slowly his tongue made its way from his own mouth, sliding into hers with the same gradual exploration. Again he sensitized her by degrees, touching first her lips, running around their soft inner sides before exploring the even line of her teeth and, at last, the deep warm recess beyond. He moved with tentative care, tempering his less patient curiosity with the belief that greed would scare her off more quickly than anything.

But he had underestimated the strength of her intuitive passion. Rather than balking at the steady invasion of his tongue, she welcomed it, granting it its lead, letting it play until she could bear no more of the exquisite torture. Then, in a rashly instinctive move, she met it with her own and their mouths mated wildly until it was Russ who reached his limit.

Tearing his mouth from hers, he moaned aloud and crushed her fiercely to his hard, throbbing body.

"Your knee!" she gasped.

"Not quite," he groaned.

His husky declaration brought her fully to her senses. Only then did Dana grow aware of how far they'd come. She had no

145

idea how her arms had reached his back, knew only that they clung to his vibrant muscles with a fierceness matching that of his arms about her back. Pressed flush to him, she knew of his hardness, of his aching need against her own. His arousal was too obvious to be missed. And she was too much of a woman not to realize the true source of his agony.

Dragging her arms from his back, she wedged them between their bodies, forced them up against his chest and levered herself back. Reality sped in to fill the space, and her eyes shot to his in horror. The extent of her fascination terrified her. She'd been so enthralled by his lovemaking that the facts of her life had momentarily escaped her. Oh, yes, he had a physical weakness. He was not the flawless male specimen she'd suspected at first. But she had her own flaw, a long-running, far-reaching one. Though he didn't yet know of it, he most certainly would if she continued along the route she'd been so recklessly taking.

She was torn between desire and fear. Under the pressure, her eyes filled with tears. Her body stiffened. She forced her chin to her chest.

"Please, Russ," she whispered beseechingly. "My keys . . . please." She was prepared to run the distance home and back with a spare if he didn't hand them over himself.

He sensed it. Crooking a finger beneath her chin, he forced her face back up. Her eyes confirmed it. With a ragged sigh he stepped back, reached into his pocket, and easily extracted the keys. As he watched her run to the door and out, though, he couldn't be upset. She'd yielded. For those few electric moments he'd conquered her fear. She'd gone soft in his arms, had let him kiss her, had even given rein to her desire and kissed him back. He would be in her blood now, just as she was in his. This certainly wasn't goodbye. To the contrary, their relationship had just begun.

Over the course of the next few weeks Dana was to come to understand this as he had. She vacillated between relief at what she'd thought to be a timely escape and dire frustration with the memory that remained. It was a memory that gnawed at her insides, a hunger pang that neither food nor work nor running could assuage. She knew the remedy;

it was no mystery. Had things been different, had she been as normal as other women, she'd have been back in Russ's arms with no holds barred.

For she'd felt it. Much as she'd tried to deny it to him, there was something special between them. She'd never been as comfortable in a man's arms. She'd never been as swept up onto a higher plane as she'd been in his embrace. Perhaps they were fated to be together. Yet there was still her problem. How did the supposed celestial matchmaker figure that into the scheme? Russ Ettinger, bad knee and all, didn't deserve a woman who might, for no logical reason, dissolve at any moment into fits of wheezing. She desperately wanted to be the whole woman for him, to have him see her as such. But if she saw him again and the . . . thing happened, he'd know. She didn't think she could bear it. More than she ever had in her entire afflicted life, she grew to resent her asthma.

The days passed and February arrived. Life went on as it always had. Yet something was different. She found herself giving greater thought to what Liz had said, found herself wondering what she might be missing. In the past she'd studiously avoided thought of men in the sense of husband, of lover. Russ Ettinger had rocked the boat. He'd made waves in the deceptively calm surface of the small pond that was her very existence.

With back-to-back snowstorms, running was that much more of a challenge. But she welcomed it. If anything, she pushed herself even harder, growing blatantly defiant of any threat to her health, running as much to vent her anger as to try to relieve herself of the coiling tension within.

She knew she'd see Russ again, knew he wouldn't give up as easily as his initial absence might suggest. It was simply a question of where and when. She tried to steel herself, to decide what to do in a rational frame of mind. But nothing about her feelings toward Russ seemed rational any longer. And the longer she went without seeing him, the less rational she became. By the time he showed up at the library late on a blustery Tuesday morning, the sight of him was as much of a relief to her starving senses as the strongest shot of adrenaline had ever been to her lungs.

He stood at the door and looked at her, wondering how he'd managed to stay away as long as he had. But he knew. He felt it in the long, drawn-out tension of his body. Cold showers had helped, as had the memory of the fear in her eyes. And then there were those other memories, of the warmth of her mouth, the sweetness of her breath, the silky flow of her hair across his hands. She was worth it. If playing it cool meant that he might slowly, gradually, get through to her core, he could be as cool as the former ladies' man had ever been.

Funny, he mused, though, how uncool he felt just then. His heart thudded. His palms grew damp. He wondered if his knee would turn perverse and give out on him as he covered the distance from the door to her desk. Some ladies' man . . .

Tucking his hand into the pocket of his sheepskin jacket for lack of anything better to do with it, he started forward. She was busy signing out books, but she'd seen him. Their eyes had met for one stunning instant. Would she be angry? After all, he hadn't made any effort to call her. Perhaps she'd been relieved that he hadn't called, preferring to pretend that that kiss had never happened. He came to a halt at the desk and waited with every last bit of his patience for

her to finish. In truth he was far from idle.
His eyes studied her face, taking in the faint
flush on her cheeks, the alluring moistness
of her lips. He saw her fumble once, then
again, trying to lift a library card from the
flat desktop with fingers that wouldn't coop-
erate. Her flush deepened as she finally suc-
ceeded.

Patience or no, it seemed forever before
the two library patrons were taken care of
and left. Dana looked up at Russ then, feeling
nooks and crannies of sensitivity come to life
all over her body. Any fears that might have
haunted her over her own inadequacies were
forgotten. He'd come! She felt strong and
suddenly all-powerful.

"May I help you?" she asked, her voice
airy, a mischievous smile spreading over her
lips.

It was the most gratifying thing he'd ever
seen. "Uh . . ." He cleared his throat. "Uh,
yes. I, uh, I'm from the other side of the
mountain and I was wondering if I might get
information on local eating spots."

"Eating spots?" she asked, noting how
handsome he looked in his white Shetland
sweater and brown corduroy slacks, his hair
neatly combed, his jaw fresh-shaven and

ruddy from the wind, the collar of his open coat rakishly shielding the back of his neck.

He cocked his dark head to the side. "You know, lunch-type spots." Then he lowered his voice to a conspiratorial whisper. "You see, there's this woman I want to take out. And I'd really like to impress her. I'd like something"—he gestured with his hand—"something quiet and relaxing, something with an atmosphere conducive to talking."

"Talking? Just talking?" she asked, delicately testing the waters.

"Well, I do want food. Something light. She's not a heavy eater. Kind of a frail-looking thing. There's even a chance she won't be able to spare much time, so I'll need a place close by."

Dana grimaced, only half in humor. "Frail?"

"Thought that'd get you," he crooned, then grew more earnest. "How about it? Lunch?"

"Now?" she whispered.

He shrugged. "I can wait. There's plenty to keep me busy around here."

Dana looked at her watch, making the decision before something sane within her could deny it. "Can you give me fifteen minutes?"

"I can give you fifty."

"Fifteen's all I need." She looked down at the pile of magazines and newspapers before her. "I have to log these in and get some information for one of the high school teachers. Then I'll be free. You could wait in the reading room."

Unwilling to push his luck, he nodded and moved off. This time, though, he found a seat in the reading room that offered him free view of her desk. And her. And he looked, enjoying the sight, making no pretense whatsoever of interest in the magazine on his lap.

Dana felt his gaze as clearly as if he'd remained standing at her desk watching her work. She tried to concentrate, to focus on what she was supposed to be doing, but all she could think about was her easy agreement to his invitation. There was reason, she told herself steadily. Perhaps, spending time with him—a harmless lunch, just talking, for example—she might find him not so intriguing after all. What she needed was something to burst the bubble of fascination her mind had blown around him in the days since she'd seen him last. That was why she was going to lunch with him. That, and nothing more.

They ate at a small restaurant, a quiet sandwich and salad haven not far from the library. "Nice place," Russ complimented her on her choice when they'd arrived and been seated. "Do you eat here often?"

"I don't usually take the time. And in weather like this, it's sometimes easier to eat in the librarians' lounge." Not that she'd minded braving the cold today, with Russ's strong arm about her shoulder to shield her from the wind. "Things must be busy at West Ridge with all this snow."

"The snow's great. It's the wind we can do without." He grimaced. "We had to shut down the upper lifts for the day. With the wind chill factor so low, hanging up there in midair for a ten-minute ride can be harrowing and a sure invitation to frostbite."

"I hadn't realized . . ."

"You've never skied, even living here all your life?"

"No. I wanted to as a child, but my parents, well, as I said, they tend to be overprotective." She felt guilty for blaming it all on them, but it was preferable to going into that more condemning explanation.

"It's a shame. Skiing is a great sport." He would have gone on, but feared he'd betray himself. As was very obvious to him now, Dana knew nothing of his more illustrious past. He rather liked it that way. How often he'd dated women who were more impressed with his athletic accomplishments than they were with him. And since his days of athletic accomplishments were over . . . "You must be an only child," he began, "for your parents to be so protective."

"Actually I've got an older brother. Max is an attorney."

Russ frowned, searching his mind in response to the bell that had rung. "Maxwell Madison, the prosecutor?"

Her eyes lit up. "You know him?"

"I know *of* him. Anyone in this state who doesn't must be deaf, dumb, and blind. He did quite a job on the Forenzia case. You must be very proud."

She grinned. "I am. We all are. He's the bright star in the family."

"But certainly not the most beautiful," he returned without pause. "I doubt you'd take a back seat on any score."

Though the compliment brought a gentle flush to her cheeks, Dana couldn't help but feel it to be ill-deserved. Again, though, she couldn't elaborate. It was far safer to simply let it go by. "How about you, Russ? You've got a sister, Danielle's mother. Any others?"

"Another sister. She's in Colorado."

"Was that where you grew up?"

He eyed her cautiously. "How did you know?"

"It was only a guess. You don't sound like a native. You've got an accent."

"Now, wait a minute." His lips twitched at the corners. "It's *you* who has the accent. Not that I hold it against you."

"Generous."

Their banter was interrupted by the waitress, who took orders for one super-size roast beef sandwich, one spinach salad, a side of potato skins to share, and a carafe of wine.

"A *carafe*?" Dana gave a hoarse whisper as the waitress moved off. "Russ, I've got to work this afternoon."

He grinned magnanimously. "Then I'll drink it."

"That's fine. I can get us back to the library, but who'll drive you home?"

"I've got nothing that desperately needs to be done. I'll sit in a corner of your library guzzling coffee until I can see straight."

"That'd be cute. The little ladies would be appalled, not to mention my boss."

"Your boss? I thought you were the boss."

"Uh-uh. There's a woman over me, though she divides her time among several libraries in the county. She's here today, so watch out."

With the arrival of the carafe of wine, Russ paused to pour them each a glass. Grasping his by the stem, he turned it, as though scanning a crystal ball. "Would you like to be the boss?" he asked speculatively.

"Me?" she exclaimed, then hesitated, finally shrugged. "I don't know. I've never really given it much thought. Why do you ask?"

It was his turn to shrug. "I guess it just came out. I'm a naturally competitive person." Indeed, he always had been, and the particular character trait had caused him much frustration in recent years. He supposed he'd mellowed with age and necessity, yet here he'd put Dana on the spot. "It's not important, really. It was wrong of me to make that assumption. What I think I truly wanted to know were your plans for the future. Do you have any aspirations, any dreams?"

"Dreams? Lots of them. Aspirations? Those are more tricky. I think I prefer to take it a day at a time rather than to have a world of unreachable aspirations."

Russ's brows lowered with his frown. "That's the second time you've put yourself down by implying limited abilities. Why, Dana? It doesn't make any sense."

She thought for a minute, sipping her wine, and struggled to find the words. "Maybe that's just one of our differences. You're a competitor. I'm not. I'm very happy with the life I lead. I don't know what the future holds. At some point I may want a different job; if so, I'll worry about it then. I'm very grateful for what I have, for what I've been able to do."

Thinking first of the fear he saw so often in her eyes, he wanted to ask if she was afraid of doing more. But that would imply a subtle pressure on his part, a disapproval of what she was now. And nothing could have been further from his sentiments. In truth he was envious. She did seem outwardly happy, content with her life. That odd shimmer of fear seemed its only blemish.

Their food arrived, momentarily diverting the conversation to lighter topics. But

Dana, too, had questions in mind. It didn't take long for them to surface.

"Did you ever run competitively?" When Russ's head shot up, she qualified herself. "I mean, I know that your knee is tricky, but if you've got that competitive drive . . ."

His jaw was taut. "I outgrew it, at least with regard to participatory athletics. I used to race. Skiing. Then I hurt myself. It was an early and enforced retirement, so to speak."

"You sound bitter," she mused softly, then regretted she'd been so vocal.

Russ didn't. He felt relieved, in a strange way, that a part of the story was coming out. Though he didn't care to have her know the details of his achievements, the fact of competition had played so heavily in his life that he felt perhaps she ought to know.

"I was the only son, the oldest child in my family. From a very early age my parents encouraged me to do things."

"They pushed you?" It was a novel thought, something totally foreign from her own experience.

"*Push* would be too harsh a word. If anyone pushed me, it was myself. My parents were always there, though, supporting me in whatever I did. Sports were my thing from the start—first hockey, then tennis, then skiing. As a kid growing up in the Rockies, it was a foregone conclusion, I suppose." He studied the swirl of wine in his glass, then took a slow sip. "At my parents' insistence, I came east to go to Bowdoin." He gave an indulgent chuckle. "I guess they did push me on that score. They were worried that skiing had become my be-all and end-all. And it had. Even the change of scenery didn't help much. I very quickly discovered the northern New England mountains, and in spite of the pressure of college, skiing continued to be my life. I endured classes for the sole moment of release, when I could break out and return to the slopes. I lived and breathed the sport, seven days a week. I was going to be the best. . . ." His words trailed off, his gaze distant.

Dana held her breath. "And then?"

After a moment's hovering suspense he let out a long sigh of defeat and stared at his mountain of a sandwich as though it were the insurmountable obstacle. "And then it was over. Everything I'd wanted was suddenly and irrevocably out of reach. I was furious."

She couldn't see it in his eyes, the anger reborn. "At yourself?"

"At everyone and everything! It was my

parents' fault for allowing my obsession with the sport to exist, my friends' fault for cheering me on so faithfully, my skis' fault for letting me veer off course, the mountain's fault for being so God damned icy." He took a breath, then released it in a long, slow *whoosh*. "I was angry at the world."

Eyes wide in astonishment, Dana stared at him. She knew what he felt. She knew it! Granted, the circumstances were entirely different. In Russ's instance it had been his knee; in hers it was a chronic case of asthma. In his instance he'd had everything, then been denied it; in her instance, she'd been denied it from the start. But the end result was the same—that ungodly anger with a bitter aftertaste.

She wanted to tell him the truth of her own circumstance, if only to offer compassion with unchallenged legitimacy. But she couldn't. She just couldn't.

"I'm sorry," she whispered, addressing her own thoughts.

His gentle smile broke the oppression of the moment. "Don't take it to heart, Dana. At least I can't blame you. It all happened very long ago. I've come to terms with it for the most part."

"How? How did you?" she asked for reasons of her very own.

"I found other things I could do, other things that mattered to me." He chose his words with care. "I was able to invest in the building of West Ridge. It was nothing when I first came here—a single chain lift and seven trails, with the potential for ten times that. We've almost made it. There are twelve lifts now, and fifty-three trails. West Ridge has come to easily rival Sugarbush, Killington, and Stowe." He chuckled at his words. "I do tend to see things through competive eyes still."

"There's nothing wrong with that."

"You're not that way. I think you're probably happier for it."

"Happier?" She thought of the years she'd ached to do so many of the things he'd done, of the times she'd have given anything in the world for that one unsteady glide across the ice on skates. "Or is the old adage true—that it's better to have loved and lost than never to have loved at all?"

There was a sudden poignancy in Russ's gaze, making Dana wonder at her choice of expression. But she'd spoken freely from the heart. Indeed, much of the reasoning behind her decision to break out four years before related to a similar sentiment. She'd simply grown tired of watching the world go by; she'd wanted to try living herself. There had always been the risk that she wouldn't make it. But she'd been determined. That determination had been a most powerful force in her favor. And she had made it, so far, at least. As for the future, and those aspirations she'd denied possessing? There were fragments of ideas and inklings of thoughts strewn about in her mind. When they materialized into things more concrete and directed, she'd know. In that sense she did live a day at a time. She preferred it that way.

Russ's voice broke into her meanderings, its tone as deep as her thoughts. "Your face is amazing, do you know that?"

"My face?" She cast him a look of amused inquiry. "How so?"

"It shows everything. Just now a wide gamut of emotions passed across it one by one." He arched a brow. "Whatever the battle you waged just then, it's been resolved, hasn't it?"

"In its way. And you really saw?" When he nodded, she raced on, feeling uncomfortably vulnerable. "I'd better watch it. At this rate, you'll know my thoughts before I do."

"I doubt that," he stated, feeling that she had to be the most self-contained, the most together woman he'd ever met. If not for that strange, inexplicable fear. But he'd get to the bottom of it—slowly but surely. He was determined.

They ate quietly for a while, each pondering private thoughts. But it was a companionable silence soon broken by talk of best-selling novels and, in particular, a recent television serialization of one. Then, following steaming cups of coffee, he returned her to the library.

"Thanks, Russ. It's been lovely." Indeed it had, far more so than she might have wished.

Likewise, his grin was too endearing for comfort. It stuck with her long after its accompanying words, "Thank you, pretty lady. I've enjoyed myself," had drifted into silence with his departure.

He made no mention of the future.

Three days later, when he appeared out of the blue at the door of the library again, though, they picked up where they'd left off. It was as if there had been no time, no agonizing in-between. Both knew differently. Both put those darker hours out of mind.

"Is it a frustration being around the store, with talk of racing all the time?" Dana asked as they sat in a booth awaiting pizzas with double cheese, sausage, pepper, and onion. "The fellow who helped me when I bought my sneakers seemed to be up on the local road races. I assume many of your customers must be, too."

"A frustration?" He folded his hands on the table before him. "Not really. I never did run competitively, for public recognition, that is. I guess you'd call me a fun runner. Running is a kind of therapy for me. If I compete, it's only against myself. You know, see how long the knee holds out."

She was about to chide him when she caught the teasing glint in his eye. Its directness made her blush. She forced herself to say something, anything to divert him. "What's been your limit? How many miles?"

"There have been days when I've done ten. It's more usually between six and eight." He seemed faintly discouraged.

"But that's great! Certainly more than my four or five a day."

"Have you ever tried adding to it?"

"No, no. Not really." She tried to sound nonchalant, shook her head, crinkled up her nose. "I don't have all that much more time to run. Besides, I'm probably one of those people with, uh, fast-twitch muscle fibers."

He laughed aloud. "Fast-twitch fibers? Where did you learn about those?"

"I work in a library," she reminded him good-naturedly. "That mean loads of goodies to bring home for evening reading."

"And you've read all there is to read about running?"

"Not all. But I have read a lot of what's on our shelves."

"And you've decided that you've got fast-twitch muscle fibers."

"Uh-huh. Ah, the food." She watched as the pizza was put down on the table.

"Hungry?" he asked. When she nodded, it seemed the signal for them to dig in. Much later the conversation resumed. "How's the week been?"

She took a last sip of her Coke. "Not bad. Yours?"

"Likewise."

"How's your niece?"

"Giving my sister migraine headaches. They're going through a tough stage, those

two. Danielle's decided that she's more interested in her boyfriend than in just about anything else. Sondra not only disapproves of
that particular boyfriend, but of the attitude
as well. It makes for a certain . . . perversity,
on both their parts."

"It's the stage. Don't you think?"

"I don't know. You're the woman. Did you
go through it when you were Danielle's age?"

If only. "Not quite," she mused wryly.

"Why not? Surely you fell in love at least
once or twice in high school."

"Not quite."

"Three times?"

She simply shook her head. Puppy love
was something that, like skiing and skating
and riding a bike, had been unthinkable.

"Come on, Dana." Russ couldn't believe
it. "With your looks I bet the boys were
always after you."

"I was fat." She tossed in a passable
excuse, announcing it with the kind of brava-
do that came from having conquered the
problem for good.

"Go on." He chided her in disbelief.

"I was. Well, not that terribly fat perhaps.
But certainly pudgy. I wore glasses nearly all
the time and kept my nose buried in a book. I

went to school; I came back home. A social life? Not exactly."

"When did things change?"

"You mean, when did I lose weight?"

"If one thing"—meaning weight—"goes with the other"—meaning a social life, "yes."

Dana addressed herself to the former. "When I started running. Four years ago."

"What made you start?"

"I, uh, I decided that I needed the exercise. You know, with old age setting in and all."

He snorted his opinion of her quip, but seemed to buy her wish for exercise. She was eternally relieved. But, then, he'd have no cause to doubt her. And exercise had been one of the reasons, albeit a secondary one, for her running.

"So you just"—he made a sweeping gesture with his hand—"went out one day and ran?"

"Oh, I did all sorts of reading beforehand. There's a way to start running . . . and there's a way to start running. I wanted to do it right."

"Slowly."

"Uh-huh. Ten minutes running to twenty minutes walking for the first few days, then fifteen and fifteen, then twenty and ten." That was what she'd read. In reality, given the fragile state of her lungs, she'd had to start even slower. It had been more like one minute running to five minutes walking, then two to ten, five to fifteen, and on up at a snail's pace. Even then she'd had initial set-backs, when, wheezing, she'd had to stop and wait. But she'd been stubborn and dead set on succeeding. Before long she'd attained that ten-to-twenty beginner's ratio. It had been a victory.

Now, feeling both guilty that she couldn't tell Russ the truth and embarrassed that she, of all people, had presumed to outline the proper breaking-in technique to a man as physically adept as he, she blushed. "I don't know why I'm telling you this. I'm sure you know far more than I."

"I don't have the resources of the library at my fingertips."

"Anyone can use the library."

"I don't have a card for yours," he reminded her with a mischievous twist of his lips. "I'm an, uh, outsider."

"Uh-huh," she drawled facetiously. "And you'll never know what you're missing. My library card is the most used card I carry."

"You have a library card? I don't believe you. Librarians don't need library cards."

"Sure they do."

"You're kidding me."

"Would I kid you?" Reaching into her purse, she extracted her wallet, from which she next ferreted out the card that had, indeed, seen better days. She held it up. "See?"

"I see."

He certainly had. Dana was not to know precisely how much until the next day, Saturday, at six thirty in the morning when she left the house to run. Loping easily down the drive, she turned onto the main street, caught sight of a familiar maroon Mazda, and came to an abrupt halt. As she stared, Russ slowly unfolded himself from the car and motioned her alongside.

"Come on. That was perfect timing. Let's go."

"What are *you* doing here?"

"Running." He was obviously dressed for it, wearing his hat and gloves and an all-weather running suit.

"But how did you know . . ." She'd rolled out of bed a mere ten minutes before. It was still too early for deep thought. For the life of her, she couldn't remember having given him her address.

To her chagrin, Russ seemed far more awake than she. "Your library card. I'm sneaky that way."

She recalled how he'd tucked her car keys into his inner pocket that morning not so long ago, and she sent him a chiding glower. She hadn't wanted him to come here! It made their relationship seem that much more—real. While he had done nothing more than drop randomly by at the library, she'd been able to tell herself that there was a certain distance, a margin of safety. It was self-deception in its purest form, yet it had given her some defense from the fear of involvement. Now though . . . here . . .

Reading her anguish, Russ closed the small distance between them and gently took her shoulders. "I thought it might be fun to run together. That's all." He gave a crooked smile. "Just think. I can protect you from anyone who might harass you."

And who would protect her from him? She refrained from asking, clearly recalling a similar discussion once before. Reluctant to get into all that again, she shrugged.

"It's really very safe," she told herself aloud, breaking into an easy stride, trying to pretend she was as alone as she'd always been.

Russ was right beside her. "You've never been heckled?"

She shook her head, intent on centering her concentration on the road ahead. "I've read about all kinds of things but, no, I haven't had any trouble. If anything, the people who pass are friendly. Not that there are many who pass on these roads at this hour."

She lapsed into silence, thinking how alone the two of them were, how—ill-advised as it was—she felt a strange inner excitement, how unfairly tall and good-looking Russ was, how natural his stride. She felt a momentary wave of self-consciousness, a fleeting few instants when she wondered what Dana Madison was doing running alongside as athletic a man as Russ Ettinger. Never in her wildest dreams had she imagined herself in such company.

As though drawn by her thoughts, Russ chose that moment to dart her a glance. "Short-twitch fibers? You do very well."

"We've only just begun. I do fine on the short distance."

"You do fine, period. You're talking."

She chuckled. "I've read that it's a good

sign, that a runner should be able to talk if he's pacing himself properly. I've never tried it before."

"You always run alone?"

"Uh-huh." The smile she slanted up at him was decidedly sheepish. "When I first ran, I was mortified at the thought of anybody seeing me, much less another runner. I was sure I looked absurd."

"You don't. You look perfect."

The excitement she already felt just running with him began to intensify with his compliment. Their eyes met and held for a heart-stopping moment. It took Dana every bit of the self-command she possessed to tear hers away.

Seeing the battle and its outcome, Russ yielded to the silence of the morning, letting its peacefulness calm her, as it did him. He marveled at the satisfaction he felt running quietly with this woman. He, too, had usually run alone, working out his frustration on the hard surface of the road. Now, strangely, he felt no frustration, at least not of the variety he'd lived with for years. His present frustration related solely to Dana, and the fact that he wanted far more of her time than the few stolen moments he'd so carefully plotted.

The road was theirs, with no more than an occasional car passing by. The air was crisp and invigorating, the rhythmic slap of their running shoes a lulling symphony. Neither runner cared that the day slowly rising was overcast. Nor was the February breeze a factor; steadily building body heat compensated for it well.

"Nice, isn't it?" Russ reflected aloud.

Dana seemed to know intuitively what he meant. "Mmm." She tipped her head up. "The sense of power, of freedom . . ." It was everything running meant to her. "Hey, I thought you said you were an evening person."

He grinned. "I am. I was. Hell, I don't know. It's not so bad getting up at this hour. Kind of different."

"You're a late sleeper?"

"You bet."

"Late nights?"

He gave her question several moments' thought before answering. "Actually, not so many lately. I'm getting to be more of a homebody than I used to be." Much as it surprised him, it was true. "I've been bringing paperwork home from the store to do at night. It's good for an evening's entertainment."

Mention of the store evoked her curiosity. "Good Sport is in several locations now, isn't it?"

"Four. We're working on a fifth to open this spring."

"Then you're pleased with its success?"

"Totally. Stunned, in fact. When I opened the first, I expected it to remain a one-outlet store. In some ways it was just a hobby. I can't believe how well it's been received in the area."

"An idea whose time has come?"

"Guess so."

They ran on, turning, at Russ's tactful suggestion, very close to the spot where Dana normally did. "But you usually go farther," she protested, feeling guilty at slowing him down.

"I usually run at night," he drawled. "It'll take some time to adjust. Like jet lag?"

Dana knew he was simply being diplomatic, that morning or evening, he could run much farther. She also sensed that he intended additional morning runs, and she grew faintly uneasy.

Russ's mind ran a similar route. "If I'd called you and suggested we run together, would you have?"

She answered softly but truthfully. "Probably not."

"Why, Dana?" His pace slowed with the diversion of his attention. "Has it bothered you this morning running with me?"

"No."

"Would you mind doing it again?"

She tried to feign nonchalance with a shrug and an even tone of voice. "You can run where you want. I haven't got a monopoly on any given stretch of the road."

"That wasn't what I asked. I asked if you'd mind if I ran with you again."

She knew what he'd asked. She'd simply tried to avoid a direct answer. For that meant taking a stand on Russ Ettinger. A nay would be a victory for the part of her that believed herself to be no match for him, for the part of her that knew she was, and always would be, an asthmatic, for the part of her that never wanted this man, of all people, to know of the weakness. A yea, on the other hand, would be a victory of the heart, which was inexplicably drawn to him, and of the body, likewise so. Infatuation—was that what she felt? What else could explain the fact that more and more lately he filled her thoughts? She daydreamed. She imagined what it might be like, and once more she was frightened.

Taking her elbow in the firm grip of his hand, he came to an abrupt stop and brought her around to face him. "There it is again. You're afraid of me. Why?"

She gulped down a breath. "I—I just don't want to get involved."

"You already are."

Three simple words. All true. Dana wanted nothing more at that moment than to melt into him. "Please, Russ," she pleaded in a whisper, "give me time." Not that it would help, but she didn't know what else to say with his deep brown eyes caressing her as they were and his nearness more heat-producing than the physical activity he'd interrupted. His hand gently stroked her cheek and she leaned into it helplessly.

"I'll try," he murmured hoarsely. "But it's not easy." He ran his thumb along the curve of her lips, sending a shiver of anticipation through her. "You're cold. Come on. Let's get you home."

She didn't bother to correct his misinterpretation of her shiver. Nor did she make a move to keep him longer when, at her house again, he ducked back into his car. When he shot her a fast "Same time tomorrow?" though, she wavered for only an instant before smiling and nodding.

On Sunday morning she had fresh coffee ready for their return. On Monday she had doughnuts, on Tuesday homemade blueberry muffins. By Wednesday, though, she was nearly out of her mind. He hadn't kissed her once.

SIX

How about dinner tonight?" he asked as they sat at her kitchen table Thursday morning sharing a last rasher of bacon. "I know you've got to work late, but I could wait here while you dress now, drop you at the library, then pick you up later so you won't have to worry about your car. You don't really want to come home at eight to fix dinner, do you?"

A date. He was actually asking her out! Before she could stop herself, she accepted. That was before she spoke with Liz.

It was late in the morning when she picked up her phone. "Circulation."

"Rusty Ettinger."

"Liz, is that you?" They'd long since shelved their differences over Dana's motivations and aspirations.

"It would have killed me until I remembered! I was just reading the local paper, an article about plans for next year's Olympic trials, and there was the name, clear as day. Rusty Ettinger was a champion skier a while back. He was headed for the Olympics before he wiped out in a pre-trial race." When she paused for a breath, she became acutely aware of a silence at the other end of the phone. "Dana, are you there?"

"I'm here," she answered in a small voice, one commensurate with her feelings at that moment.

"Well, what do you think? Isn't that exciting?"

"Exciting? That's one word for it!" Humiliating was a second, intimidating a third, angering a fourth. It was the last that gave force to her words.

"Why are you angry?"

"He could have told me."

"He told you he skied."

"Sure. But never quite the extent of it."

"Dana, it's nothing to be angry about. I mean, he must have had his reasons." She grasped at the possibilities. "Maybe it bothers him that he can't race anymore. Maybe he's put it all behind him. Maybe he wanted you to accept him purely for what he is now. Maybe he even suspected you'd feel uncomfortable."

"Uncomfortable? Hmph! That's putting it mildly."

"And what do you have to feel uncomfortable about?"

"Liz, if he is what you say," and given his own sketchiness on the topic it more than was probable, "he's a celebrity. Do you know how dumb I feel next to him, not to mention having been so far out of the sports scene that I didn't even recognize his name?"

"So what? If he's gone so far as to ask you out, he must not mind. And besides, you're into the sports scene now. What difference does the past make?"

"It makes a difference to me." And that was the crux of it. She cleared her throat. "Listen, Liz, I've got to run. Can I talk with you later?"

"Sure. Hey, when did you say you were seeing him again?"

"I didn't. But we're having dinner tonight."

"Have fun."

"Yeah."

It seemed like wishful thinking. By the

time Russ innocently sauntered into the library shortly before eight, she was ready to explode. Greeting him with a tight smile, she took longer than usual to gather together her things, feeling perverse satisfaction at keeping him waiting, answering his initial attempts at conversation with terse replies. It was inevitable that he turn to her when at last they were in the privacy of his car.

"Okay, Dana. Let's have it. What's wrong?" He made no move to start the engine.

Dana looked at him then, the first time she'd directly done so since he'd arrived to pick her up. "Why didn't you tell me, Russ? Champion skier. Olympic contender. Why didn't you tell me?" Mixed in with anger was a large dose of hurt.

Had she been able to see his face clearly, she would have seen its color drain away. The darkness held all from her but the reflection of the dim dashboard light in his eyes.

"It's not important," he stated blandly.

"Not important? My God, it puts you in a totally different league. I should have known."

Russ tried to make out her expression,

but it was as ill-lit as his own. "That's funny," he began, not at all amused, "but I really thought it wouldn't matter to you. I thought you'd be above that kind of thing."

"Above?" She felt miles below him at that point. "You're mocking me."

"I'm dead serious," he said and he was throughly discouraged as well. "I don't ski any longer, at least not in any competitive way. So what does it matter that I used to be good? That's all in the past."

She shook her head, barely hearing his words, too enmeshed in her own torment to be aware of his. "It's you. Don't you see? It's a vital part of your past, a fantastic achievement. I can't forget—"

"Stop it, damn it!" he roared in a sudden eruption of anger that rivaled, no, surpassed her own. "I'm sick of hearing about it! It's behind me. I can't do it anymore. And if you think that knowledge doesn't eat at me, you're crazy. Why can't you all just let the past rest?"

It was Dana's turn to be taken aback, emerging very slowly from a self-centered anger. She'd been focused on her own insecurities. Now she heard something different. "What?"

"My racing days are over! Over! But you and everyone else around here, it seems, refuse to accept that. Do you have any idea how . . . how humiliating it is to be referred to as a champion when I can't even trust my knee to get me down the easiest run?"

"That wasn't what I—"

"Don't give me that," he interrupted sharply. "I've been through this too many times to be fooled." He faced front and stared out the windshield. Even the dark couldn't hide the taut disillusionment chiseled into his profile. "I'm so tired of being judged on standards I just can't meet anymore. When I realized that you hadn't recognized my name, I actually was relieved. I felt free for the first time in years." He gave a bitter laugh. "That was a pipe dream—thinking you wouldn't care even if you did know."

"But—"

"Spare me the protests," he gritted out, one hand choking the wheel, the other reaching for the ignition. "I think I'd better take you home."

"I don't want to go home!" she fairly screamed, unsure as to whether she was more appalled at their misunderstanding or frustrated by his seeming unwillingness to let her explain. "I don't care about your accomplishments in that sense. What you did then doesn't in the least effect the way I regard you now. It affects the way I regard *me*!"

"What are you talking about?"

The dullness of his tone disturbed her all the more. "It was bad enough when I thought you were just a super athlete. But a champion? I feel so, so inadequate beside you," she cried, her anguish coming to the surface.

The air in the car was totally still. Dana held her breath.

"Wait a minute here," Russ growled, eyeing her warily. "Are we talking about the same thing?"

"I'm talking about the fact that I'm a non-athlete and a non-competitor. I move in quieter, less illustrious circles." She paused only to gasp unevenly. "What is it you see in me? I don't want to be toyed with, Russ. Is it some kind of game? You must be used to beautiful little snow bunnies who wear sleek designer snowsuits and zip down the slopes without messing a hair, then live it up all night at some ski lodge. That's everything I've never been! I can't compare with that kind of woman. I feel foolish!"

There was a long pause then, an expectant one. When at last Russ spoke, his voice was as quiet and as gentle as it had ever been. "I should hope so. I certainly do."

"Wh-what?"

"Oh, Dana." He lifted a hand to lightly massage her neck. She wanted to pull away but couldn't. "I misunderstood. You misunderstood. Don't you see? I didn't tell you about my skiing past because I'm the one who feels inadequate. And because every other woman I've ever known has been so enamored with that past that she could barely see *me* through the glitter. It's glitter that's faded now though. Hell, there are times when I think I should have taken up life as an accountant in a big city where no one could make the association between what I am and what I was. It's been hard enough for me to accept my limitations, without being constantly reminded of them. With you it was different from the start. You didn't know; you could see me as me. And as for comparing you with those others," he added softly, "you're right. There's no comparison. You're so far superior."

"I'm not."

"Yes! You are! There's so much more to you than there is to any snow bunny. Damn!" With his whispered oath he drew her head firmly against his chest, wrapped his arms around her, held her as closely as the bucket seats would allow. "This is no game, Dana. I'd never hurt you. I've told you that so many times. I'd never hurt you."

Nothing had changed regarding her own feelings, her own past, yet for the moment Dana pushed them from her mind to simply enjoy this closeness. He felt so good. His chest was warm and vibrant beneath her cheek, his arms held her every bit as tightly as she craved to be held.

"Oh, Russ," she whispered, her eyes closed, her arms easily slipping beneath his coat to hug his waist. She wanted to tell him how sorry she was to have caused him those few moments of painful misunderstanding, but no further words would come to disturb these new moments of exquisite pleasure. His scent was an alluring stimulant, all male, fresh, and clean. His arms were a haven in which to delight. When she felt his lips against her hair, then her brow, she tipped her head back to meet them with her own.

He kissed her deeply, his mouth opening hers to vivid pleasure, directing it, leading it as if in a dance to ensure a sweet, sizzling syncopation. Dana followed his every step, enthralled by the firmness of his lips, their warmth, their moistness. Her tongue, lured easily from retreat by the memory of past exploration, slid the length of his and back. Even when their lips parted, those tongues demurred, keeping contact with an erotic touch, a heart-stopping curl.

The catch of her breath seemed a reminder to them both of where they were. Breathing roughly himself, Russ drew back to stare at her for one electric moment before tucking her hard against him. With her ear pressed to his heart, Dana easily heard its racing beat. His words elaborated on its message.

"God, Dana, I've wanted to kiss you again." He ran his hands up and down her spine, their touch searing even through the heavy wool of her coat. "I've wanted to hold you like this." Then he set her back so that he could see her face. "No, not like this. I take that back. I don't want it to be in a car. It should be in a very quiet place, on a rug before the fire, with soft music in the background and one shared glass of wine."

Dana found the romance in him to be as heady as his unadulterated masculinity. Looking up at him, she was overwhelmed with an emotion she could no longer ignore. Here in Russ's arms she could momentarily forget the terrors of the past. In his arms she was beautiful, healthy, whole. She wanted to be with him, to give to him, to share that single glass of wine with him. God help her, she loved him! She hadn't wanted to; she'd fought it with every possible evidence of their incompatibility. But perhaps they weren't all that incompatible after all. Perhaps their only lingering differences were in her own mind. After all, he didn't know of her asthma.

He gave her one last, sweet kiss, then set her back and cleared his throat of its huskiness. "Let's go get some dinner. Okay?"

"Okay," she whispered, relieved at the reprieve from her thoughts. She wanted to forget them, to pretend she was that whole, healthy woman Russ seemed to see her as, to simply enjoy his company while she had it.

And she did. They ate at an elegant

restaurant near the coast, one Russ had chosen as much for the drive there as for the quiet atmosphere within. If Dana knew herself to be in love, she could almost imagine him to be similarly smitten. He was warm and attentive, ever gentle and solicitous. The passionate moments they'd shared in the car lingered in the touch of his hand on her waist as they walked to their table, the subtle caress of her shoulder when he seated her, the occasional stroking of her hand as he reached for it between courses. As though he couldn't bear to have her out of his sight, his eyes left hers only to study the menu and the wine list and to acknowledge the presence of the waiter. Their concentration was focused solely on each other, until they were finishing their dessert.

It was at that point that a departing couple detoured to their table. "Russ! How are you?" the man intoned.

Wrenched back from utter distraction, Russ looked up in surprise. When he recognized the faces before him, though, he broke into a grin, stood, and extended his hand. "It's good to see you, David. Heather, hi."

"Hi, yourself, stranger," the woman replied.

At a moment's impression, Dana took in a chic wool dress, slender lines, a shoulder-length fall of thick black hair, and a face that was unarguably lovely. The man was as good-looking, tanned, and well-built, with a thatch of silver hair and a rugged face that gave him several years on Russ to compensate for the inch or two he lacked in height.

Then Russ was introducing her. "David, Heather, I'd like you to meet Dana Madison. Dana, these are my old friends, David Ahearn and Heather O'Brien. David is an M.D. with a specialty in sports medicine. Heather is a photographer with a specialty in sports, period. I've worked with both of them over the years."

Dana smiled her hellos, feeling an unwelcome wave of insecurity at the appearance of these two from Russ's other life. But Russ seemed pleased to see them and she found consequent pleasure in that. Her worries were further eased when he came to stand beside her chair and lay a proprietary hand on her shoulder.

"Sit down and have some coffee with us," he offered.

David looked at Heather. "Can you spare five more minutes?"

"Why not?"

Whereupon Russ motioned to the waiter for two more cups, then drew his own chair alongside Dana's to make room for two others to be brought from a nearby table. He seemed eager for Dana to get to know his friends, and for them to get to know her. The thought warmed her. Furthermore, her own ear had perked up at Russ's mention of David's specialty. Sports medicine. Would he be someone she could talk with?

The five minutes expanded into ten and flew quickly by, consumed by talk of West Ridge, of a conference David had recently attended in New York, of Heather's latest assignment for a renowned sports magazine. Russ deftly kept Dana in the center of the conversation, filling her in on background here and there, telling of her work and the devotion to running which it seemed David shared.

"Not me," Heather laughed. "You guys can have it! I'm happy enough to be on skis, where the force of gravity does most of the work. You don't get tired, Dana?"

"Sometimes. But it's worth it. Not that I'm universally sports-minded. This is my one and only outlet."

David asked how long she'd been running and how far she went. It was Russ who picked up from there, knowing his friend well enough to anticipate the next question.

"Don't ask her if she races, David. She claims to be a non-competitive soul." Then he turned to Dana. "David's won any number of races. Last year he finished third in the Maine Coast Marathon."

"Forty to forty-nine-year division. You've got to mention that," David chided.

"That's wonderful!" Dana exclaimed. "Have you always been a racer?"

David chuckled. "That's the joke of it. I was totally non-athletic as a kid. To this day I can't ride a bicycle. Running seems to be the only sport in which I can manage to coordinate myself. But, to answer your question, no, I haven't always raced. I kind of fell into sports medicine when Russ needed a doctor on call at West Ridge. It was then that I became fascinated with the problems of athletes, particularly the ability many have of overcoming aches and pains for the sake of keeping active and strong. The people I met were an inspiration. I took up running ten years ago and have been an addict ever since."

There was far more to his story that

Dana wanted to hear, and a wealth of questions she wanted to ask. But the talk veered away and it was just as well. Her questions could never be asked here, in this company. Silently she filed what information she could on David's practice. With no justification for it at all, she felt strangely encouraged.

During the ride home from the restaurant, she couldn't help but pump Russ for information. "David is remarkable. The field of sports medicine is *in*. He must be very much a part of it to be attending conferences and all."

"Uh-huh."

She tried to sound nonchalant. "Where are his offices?"

"He's in a medical building three blocks from the store."

"You must see him often."

"Not that often. He's busy."

"Has he ever treated your knee?"

"He tried." He reached over for her hand and brought it in his back to his thigh. His thoughts were centered on this woman beside him, on how warm her fingers were against him, on how she'd come to life in his arms earlier. The last thing he wanted to discuss was his knee . . . or David Ahearn.

Dana couldn't help herself. "Is he primarily an orthopedic man?"

"I suppose. But he's branched out with the field."

She let it go for a while then, yielding to a growing awareness of the solidity of Russ's thigh, of the seductive way he held her hand to it. And then there was the after-glow of a divine dinner, even more so the memory of the kiss they'd shared earlier. In hindsight, she felt a tremor of excitement, a yearning to be everything and more for Russ. If only . . .

As they neared familiar sights, the wheels of her mind began to turn again. "It sounds as though David believes in racing."

Russ shot her a sharp glance before returning his gaze to the road. "Not for everyone. Why?"

His curtness took her by surprise. "I—I don't know. I was just wondering."

"You seem fascinated with David." Though his hand remained on hers, its movement had stilled completely.

"No, no. Just curious."

He did take his hand from hers then and gripped the steering wheel hard. "Isn't he a little old for you?"

Whipping her own hand back from his

thigh, Dana looked at him in time to catch the tight set of his profile. He was jealous! It was simultaneously a heady and disturbing thought. Though the last thing she wanted was to hurt Russ, she just couldn't tell him the truth. "I'm not interested in him. It's just that . . ."

"Just that what?"

"Just that," she groped, "that his field is intriguing."

"Sports medicine? You've got a problem?"

What he'd snapped off in a tone of near anger was a direct hit. She certainly did have a problem, two of them, in fact. And the one that concerned her now wasn't asthma. Russ was upset and she'd caused it. She'd thoughtlessly run on about David, never dreaming Russ would be bothered.

"No problem," she said quietly, then said no more. She wanted to say, Don't be jealous, it's you I love. But she couldn't. She felt inadequate enough as it was; to make such a heartfelt confession when she wasn't all that sure the sentiment was returned could only invite humiliation.

As she continued to search for the words to restore the warmth between them, Russ turned off the main road onto her drive, pulling the car to a halt by her door.

"Come in for a little while?" she ventured timidly.

"Maybe I shouldn't." He knew what he wanted, could feel it in every fiber of his being. He also knew of the surge of blind jealousy that did something ugly to desire.

"Please?"

Her soft pleading was his undoing. If she was playing games, she'd have to learn the consequences. He looked at her hard, then climbed from the car and came around to help her out. When she unlocked the front door, she glanced up questioningly. At his nod, they entered.

Tossing her coat on the nearby chair, Dana turned to him, her mouth suddenly dry. She'd hoped that by inviting him in she might get him to relax. But she didn't know where to begin. "Can I—can I get you some coffee or something?"

"I don't want coffee." Eyes glued to hers, he shrugged out of his coat and let it fall on the chair. Without wasting another word, he took her in his arms and kissed her as he never had before. His mouth plundered hers, punishing her softness with every bit of the need that had built in him over the past weeks. In his frustration he called on none of the control he'd used before, intent only on demonstrating the force of the fire Dana played with.

By rights she should have been terrified. With another man she would have fought, screamed, if not suffered a full-scale asthmatic attack. But she loved Russ. She knew he needed this outlet, knew its provocation had been her own doing. If only she'd been able to tell him the truth about her interest in David. But she hadn't. And Russ was angry. This kiss, bearing an untethered passion, was the staking of his claim on her. Fight? Scream? How could she when she wanted him so?

Tearing his lips from hers, Russ swept her off her feet and carried her to the couch. Before she could cry out even to speak of the slightest fear, he was half atop her. His hands pinioned hers on either side of her head; his mouth seized hers once more.

And suddenly Dana wasn't thinking of fear. She was thinking of the primitive nature of his onslaught and of the answering primal instinct coming to slow life within her. Her lips responded, opening to his. Her mouth took the thrust of his tongue with an odd welcome. She would have been startled at herself had she been aware of what she was doing. But minute by minute she was more swept up in his passion until her own mirrored it fully.

She'd never been kissed this way. She'd never responded this way. Everything in her life had been slow and disciplined, well-planned and properly paced. Yet she felt alive now and decidedly reckless. She suddenly ached to know all it was that she'd missed for so long.

Russ released her hands then to let his own roam over her body. It was the first time he'd touched her this way, shaping his fingers to her shoulders, her waist, her hips and thighs, branding each spot his. She found herself straining upward, craving more. When he brought his hands up to cover her breasts, she gasped against his lips, not in fear but ecstasy.

She moaned softly then and clutched his back, thrilling to the flex of his muscles as she felt her own mold to him. Under his active exploration, her breasts grew swollen. He found their tips through the silk of her blouse and rubbed them to even greater turgidity. When he fumbled impatiently with the buttons of her blouse, she was helpless to protest. When the blouse lay open and he released the front clasp of her bra, she thought she'd die with wanting him.

It was only the beginning. His fingers touched her skin, their manly roughness inching upward from her waist over the smoothest of flesh to her breasts. His lips were by her ear; she thought she heard him rasp her name before he gritted his teeth together. Then his hand settled over her fullness, massaging it in circles that continued to spiral through her body in non-ending coils.

Overwhelmed by the depth of the feelings he evoked, she closed her eyes. She felt him raise himself, felt his gaze on her, felt him lower his head to take one taut nipple between his teeth. Even his roughness was a sweet pain, diverting her mind from the growing ache deep in her belly.

Then it was over. Going suddenly still, Russ dropped his forehead to her chest. His breath came in ragged gasps, as though there were great pain mixed with passion. Eager to comfort him, to hold him closer, Dana raised her hands to his hair. But with an oath that was muffled in the valley between her breasts, he pushed himself up and away. He was on his feet, standing over her, before she understood what had happened.

Thrusting his own fingers through his hair, he looked down at her with a disdain that brought a world of reality crashing down on her. Clutching her blouse front together, she struggled to a sitting position. Tears filled her eyes.

"Russ?" she whispered brokenly. It was as though history repeated itself, except that this time the only impediments to her breathing were dissipating passion and burgeoning despair.

"I can't do this, Dana," he growled, his voice rough and gravel-edged. "Not in anger." Turning on his heel, he snatched up his coat on his way to the door, and left.

Dana sat, stunned and trembling, listening to the rev of his motor, the savage squeal of his tires on the drive. In the silence that remained after all other sound had faded into oblivion, she tried to make sense out of his abrupt exit.

It was hard when her own emotions were in a state of such utter upheaval. She was hurt that he hadn't wanted her enough to stay, humiliated to have let herself be so bared to his whim, disappointed that he'd left her so achingly unfulfilled. Her thoughts were physically oriented, as the full impact of what she'd been about to do set in.

Only with time, as the quiet of the night and the reassuring familiarity of her surroundings calmed her, did she see things more clearly. Then thoughts of the physical gave way to the more germane psychological issues.

Russ had been hurt. The force of the passion he'd unleashed on her had reflected that hurt. But he'd had the peace of mind to realize what was happening before it had reached its conclusion, and he'd withdrawn. Disdain or *self*-disdain? Past experience had primed Dana for the former, yet, as she pondered it, she became increasingly convinced it had been the latter. He'd been hurt, yes, and angry and jealous. But that wasn't how he'd wanted to take her. And, more critically to her, despite frustration's lingering ache, it wasn't how she wanted to be taken. She had to respect him all the more for sparing her the ordeal of giving herself to him under those circumstances.

Yes, his departure had been for the best. She felt far too much for him to want him to take her in anger. She wanted warmth and tenderness. She needed it. For she knew two things that he didn't. She knew that she'd had one brutal experience with a man, when she'd been reduced to a wheezing mass of humiliation on the very verge of lovemaking. And she knew that she was a virgin.

Was she actually going to try again? It was this question that remained when all others had fallen by the wayside. She'd vowed she never would, had for years let a natural fear protect her from involvement. Strange, she mused, how she'd forgotten that fear in Russ's arms. She'd been so drawn into his passion that she'd thought of nothing but seeing it through to its age-old end.

In a moment's stunning realization, it occurred to her that other than the breathlessness of passion, her lungs had been perfectly clear. She hadn't had to wheeze or gasp for air as she had that other time. She'd been free of it—free!

Might it be all right? Had those years of fright been unnecessary? But there was a key, one for which she'd groped unsuccessfully that night after her argument with Liz. It came to her now, in the dark of the night, with thoughts of Russ foremost in her mind.

The right man. That was the key. The right man might understand, might refuse to let her upset herself to the point of illness. Was Russ the right man for her?

Alex Kraft had been the wrong one. She understood that now, just as she understood the reasons why. Though she'd found him pleasant enough and reasonably attractive, she'd felt little else for him personally. At the time, she'd been rebelling against her sheltered past. She'd wanted a man. He'd been available and reasonably acceptable. She'd used Alex. He'd used her. No wonder he'd been disgusted when she'd reneged in such an elemental way on their unspoken bargain.

It was different with Russ. Everything was different with Russ. She loved him. And, particularly if his behavior of the evening—jealousy and all—had been any indication, she believed he felt something special for her in turn. Was he the right man? Could it be beautiful, as Liz had said? Could she be that whole woman for Russ?

But there was more to be done than the simple giving of her body. There was the broader issue to be considered, the fact that, lovemaking notwithstanding, she felt lacking as a person. The past evening had been an eye-opener in many ways. She knew what she had to do and, for the first time, knew how she wanted to do it.

The first order of business, she decided, was to visit David Ahearn.

SEVEN

First thing the following morning, Dana called his office. "Hello," she said in response to the sweet-toned receptionist's greeting. "I wonder if I might speak with Dr. Ahearn?" It occurred to her that he might well be with a patient. She was close.

"He's not in the office at the moment. May I ask who's calling?"

"This is Dana Madison. I'm a friend of Russ Ettinger's. I met the doctor last night." Suspecting that everything she said would be passed on to the doctor, she felt the reminder worthwhile. If she recalled everything about David Ahearn, she had good reason. What reason would he have to remember her? None at all. "Do you expect him soon?"

"He's at the hospital, in surgery," came the melodic reply. "Is this a personal call?"

"No, uh, actually it's a medical one."

"Would you like to make an appointment?"

"I—I wanted to talk with the doctor first." What she didn't want was a three-week wait for fear she'd lose her resolve. "When might I reach him?"

"He's due back in the office at eleven. Perhaps he can get back to you?"

"That would be fine." Leaving her number, Dana hung up the phone and tried to occupy herself with work as she awaited his call. The excitement she felt at what she'd decided to do was tempered only by a sense of mild apprehension, a fear that David might discourage her. She was taking a chance, she realized that. Chip Wilson had been the only doctor with whom she'd ever discussed running; he'd been negative from start to finish. This new step she wanted to take was a big one. David Ahearn's approval could make all the difference in the world.

It was shortly before eleven that her phone rang. "Reference desk."

"Dana Madison, please."

"Speaking. David?"

"That's right, Dana. I've got a message here that you called."

"Yes! And thanks for calling me back. I, uh, I wondered if I might speak with you."

"Medically?"

"Uh-huh."

"What's the matter, Dana?" he asked, concerned.

"Nothing . . . nothing urgent, that is. It's just that, well, after meeting you last night and learning of your specialty, I was hoping you might be able to give me some advice."

"About something you'd rather not discuss on the phone?"

"That's right," she admitted softly. "I was going to just call and make an appointment, but I wanted to see you soon and—"

"And you were afraid you'd be put off for a month?" he broke in, a reassuring smile warming his words.

"Something like that." She felt decidedly sheepish.

"Well, you were right!" he returned, taking her by pleasant surprise. "If you'd just made an appointment through Linda you'd probably have had at least a ten-day wait. Things have been particularly busy lately.

213

I'm glad you called me directly. How about late today?"

"Today?" She hadn't expected an appointment quite that soon. She was elated.

"I've got an appointment at five, then a break until seven, when the evening clinic begins. If you come in at five thirty, we'll have some time to talk."

"You don't mind? That won't leave you much time for supper. I hate to be an inconvenience."

"You're no inconvenience," he said with genuine conviction. "Russ is a very special friend, and you're a friend of his. If I can do anything for you, I'd be thrilled."

As delighted as she was, there was a tiny voice of discomfort within that bid her to speak up. The last thing she wanted was for David to bump into his very special friend with a Hey, guess who I saw! She spoke hesitantly. "Uh, David? The, uh, the only thing is . . ."

". . . that Russ doesn't know you're calling?"

"No." She wondered if she sounded as guilty as she felt, and was relieved when David seemed unfazed.

"And I wouldn't have told him, even if you hadn't warned me. When you said that this was a medical matter, you automatically put certain practices into effect. Among other things, I'm a firm believer in doctor-patient confidentiality. So, say five thirty?"

"Five thirty," she smiled, feeling exuberant. "Thanks, David."

In fact, she was there early, having left the library on the stroke of five to assure herself sufficient time to drive to the office, whose address she'd gleaned from the phone book. Then she sat in the waiting room, wondering if what she was doing was right, praying that no one would walk in who might remotely recognize her, finally reflecting on Russ and the way they'd parted the night before.

She hadn't heard from him. He'd neither shown up to run that morning, nor called her at the library at any point during the day. But then, she hadn't expected it. Russ struck her as a man who would have to work out his feelings on his own. And she couldn't be discouraged. After all, there had been that dinner, when everything had been beautiful between them. She refused to believe that he'd be able to forget that.

Her mind wandered to thoughts of the future, as it related to her presence here in

David Ahearn's office. Russ would be proud of her; she'd be proud of herself. But what if David said no?

As the minutes dragged, she thumbed nervously through the broad array of sports magazines on the waiting room table. Having read the latest running publications in the library, she had picked up a skiing magazine and was absently flipping through its slick pages when she halted abruptly, leafed back several, and narrowed her eyes on an advertisement. It was *his* name, *his* face! She couldn't believe it! Russ Ettinger endorsing the latest model ski boots. He hadn't told her this either. Yet now she understood why and could feel no anger. Moreover, there was a modesty about him that appealed to her. Given what he'd done in his life, he could have been an impossible egotist. How glad she was that he wasn't.

"Dana?"

At the sound of her name she looked up quickly to find David at the door of his office smiling his welcome. Flipping the magazine shut, she let it fall to the nearby table as she stood. What was between David and her had nothing to do with ski boots. And though it had everything to do with Russ Ettinger, she didn't want him to see.

"Hi, David," she murmured shyly, feeling suddenly timid before the man who now wore a proper white coat over his shirt and slacks. "Thanks so much for seeing me."

Sensing her awkwardness, David was particularly gentle. "It's my pleasure. Come on in." He stood back to let her pass into his office, then closed the door and motioned her toward a chair. When she'd taken it and he'd settled himself in turn behind his desk, he leaned forward to prop his forearms atop a brown-leather-edged blotter. "Now, tell me what I can do for you."

It seemed she'd been practicing the words all day, yet she still had trouble getting them out. She'd never before told anyone in the running world. And this was Russ's friend; perhaps she'd made a mistake in coming.

"Everything is truly confidential, Dana," David offered in soft response to the doubt written all over her face.

"I know. It's just strange to talk about it, I guess." She cleared her throat, frowned at her clenched fingers, then finally looked back at David. "You know that I've been running.

When I started four years ago, it was against my doctor's advice."

"Against? But why?"

This was the hard part. Once aired, it could never be taken back. But she knew it had to be done. The thought of all she wanted to be for Russ gave her the courage to go on. "I'm an asthmatic. I have been since I was a child."

"An asthmatic?" David's eyes lit up. "That's wonderful, Dana!"

"Wonderful?" she asked with a pained grimace.

Chuckling knowingly, he held up his hand. "I'm sorry. That came out the wrong way. My mind sometimes jumps two steps ahead of itself. What I meant to say was that I'm sorry you have asthma, but that I'm thrilled you've been running in spite of it all."

"You are?" Her own eyes matched the illumination of his. She'd just known he'd be on her side. "You can't imagine how relieved I am to hear that! I've felt like a pariah, with everyone telling me that I'm positively crazy."

"Everyone? Who's everyone?"

"Actually," she quickly qualified herself, "not that many people. My allergist, my parents, my brother—I finally decided not to mention it to anyone else."

"Russ couldn't have been against it."

Her voice softened. "I didn't know Russ back then. We only met a few weeks ago."

"Surely he doesn't think you're crazy."

Her confession was spoken slowly, with great hesitance. "He doesn't know I have asthma."

It was a sober punch line. David sat quietly pondering it for several moments, trying to put together a puzzle for which he had only half the pieces. Finally he leaned back in his chair and eyed her, bewildered. "I'm not quite sure why you've come to me."

She needed no further prodding. "I've been running on my own for four years now with no medical sanction at all. I started very slowly and have built up to four or five miles a day." The words spilled with snowballing speed. "It's been like a medicine for me; by running faithfully every day, I've been able to give up the pills I used to take every four hours. I've never felt better in my life. I've never had fewer attacks. Now what I want is to race. And I want your opinion as to whether I can do it." Having said what she'd come to say, she sat back to catch her breath.

David's smile gave her an instant shot of strength. "In case you haven't guessed it by now, I believe most anything is possible." As he spoke he drew a fresh piece of paper from his drawer and took up a pen. "I wouldn't presume to give my advice, however, until I know everything there is to know about you medically." He put pen to paper. "Let's take it from the top. How old were you when you were first diagnosed as being an asthmatic?"

The next forty-five minutes were spent with David asking and Dana answering all manner of questions concerning her health, past and present. A physical exam prompted further questions. By the time he was done, she was convinced that he knew more about her physical state than any person ever had. As for the psychological, he was well on his way to learning.

"Why, Dana? Why do you want to race?"

"It's . . . it's something else to do."

He shook his head slowly. "I don't buy that. An asthmatic doesn't buck the odds to run simply for 'something else to do.' Come on. The truth."

She eyed him solemnly then. "The truth?" It seemed a farce not to tell him; he knew so much else about her. The compassion with which he studied her was the clincher. She wanted him to know. "The truth is," she sighed, "that I need to do it, that I don't think I can feel I've really conquered this thing unless I've done it, that I want to earn my own respect so that I can be convinced of . . . of his."

"Ah. It's Russ then." It was as though he'd known it, as though he'd simply wanted to hear her say it.

But clarification was necessary. "It's me really. Russ has been the catalyst, but it's something I've got to do."

"Have you talked racing with him?"

"No!" she exclaimed, then forced her voice to a more normal pitch. "At least, not in terms of me. I wanted to be sure I could do it without having to go into long explanations to Russ."

"About your asthma?"

"Yes."

Pondering this, David grew more quiet. "What does Russ mean to you?"

She wavered, shrugging. "We haven't known each other that long." Even to this man, who now knew her so well, she couldn't confess the depth of her feelings.

"Yet it sounds as though there's something there."

She dropped her gaze. "There is. On my part, at least."

"But you don't want to tell him about this problem?"

Looking up then, she felt less sure than she had in the past. "I don't know," she whispered soulfully. "I view it as such a weakness. If I had my way, he'd never have to know."

"If your relationship is to have any future, he's got to know. I mean, you still have occasional attacks. How do you think he'd feel to see you having one and know that you hadn't had enough faith to tell him?" He watched the flow of pain on her face and prayed he was getting through. "He can handle it, Dana. I know the man. He'd never think less of you for it. If anything, he'd have that much more respect for the running you do. He appreciates that kind of thing. Don't forget, he's got his own weakness. He sees his knee as every bit as much of a blemish as you your asthma."

Her lips thinned. "So I've gathered." Russ had been more than blunt on the matter in the car last night.

"Well, it's true. And it's tough for him,

having been in the limelight once. He pushes all the time, running far more than he should."

"You're against that?" She was surprised; she'd more or less assumed David to be in favor of pushing against all odds.

"I'm against it in Russ's case. I very definitely recommend he exercise, but within limits. You see, his situation is different from yours. His knee's been permanently damaged. Not so your lungs. Mind you"—he held up a hand—"I'm not suggesting you run a marathon tomorrow. But within common sense and proper training, I think you could do anything you wanted. You're lucky, in that sense."

"Then you really do think I could race?" she asked cautiously.

"With common sense and proper training," he repeated, momentarily leaving the issue of Russ alone. "What I'd like to do"—he looked down at the notes on his desk—"is to get hold of your allergist's records."

"Chip? He may not like that."

"Don't worry. I can handle him. Then, if it's all right with you, I'd like to consult several of my colleagues." He anticipated her reaction, and hastened to reassure her.

"Confidentially, of course, though these doctors are both from the Midwest and wouldn't know either you or Russ. They're recognized authorities within the field of sports medicine on respiratory problems. I'd be curious to see what they have to say."

"What if they say no?"

"That you shouldn't run?" He shook his head. "They won't. I know these men. But they may have some interesting things to say about a training program, or medication."

"I don't want medication," she insisted. "That was one of the reasons I began to run—I was sick and tired of being a slave to those pills."

"I know, I know, Dana," he said, rising from his chair to circle the desk and perch on its corner. He was close to her, talking softly, reassuringly. "But that's where the common sense comes in. You *are* an asthmatic. You'll always *be* an asthmatic. Until modern medicine finds a cure, you're going to have to live with the affliction. Now, I agree with you. You shouldn't be taking medicine if you don't need it—and obviously you don't, if you've done so well without it. But you've got to be prepared, particularly if you're going to race. You've got to know what to expect and how to handle it. And that's where my colleagues come in. They've simply had more experience with breathing problems. After I speak with them, you and I can sit down and plot out a training program for you." There was a gleam in his eye that told of his excitement at the thought. It was instantly contagious.

"I'd like that," she smiled, rising. "But I really should be going. You've given me far more time than I deserve. I'm afraid you'll barely have time for supper."

He shot a glance at his watch, amazed at the passage of time, though not at all regretful. "It's all I'll need," he said, then stood and put an arm around her shoulder in the way of a friend. "You, Dana, deserve far more than my time. You deserve a laurel wreath for what you've done already. You're truly remarkable." He walked her to the door. "And I'd love to see you race. It'd be good for you. You're ready."

She grinned up at him. "I hope so . . . for many reasons." As David opened the door to walk her out, she had visions of going the distance and crossing that glorious finish line. Russ would be so proud. . . .

"Russ!"

At David's exclamation, she looked up, then followed his gaze across the waiting room to the outer door of the office. Russ stood on its threshold, his hands on his hips, his eyes glued to the duo emerging from the office.

"Russ!" she whispered in stunned echo. When last she'd seen him he'd been deeply agitated; he seemed no better now. Her heartbeat skidded to a halt, then raced on at double time. "What are you doing here?"

"Funny, I was just going to ask you the same thing."

"I came to see David."

"That's obvious. Did you have a nice visit?" His eyes drilled her with anger; his voice dripped of sarcasm. He walked slowly closer.

"It was a medical call, Russ," David ventured in her behalf. He had to know the awkwardness of the situation, that the last thing Dana wanted was for Russ to know she'd come. But while it was perfectly understandable that Russ would be puzzled at her presence, David hadn't expected as dark a reaction. He half suspected Russ was jealous. "And you?"

Russ's laugh was harsh and rife with self-mockery. "I was going to take you for a beer, friend, but I see you've got better company."

David dropped his arm from Dana's shoulder, leaving a hand at her waist for token support. "Dana's just leaving and I could use a beer." He cast a glance at his watch. Short as he was for time, it seemed the best solution to a difficult situation. Over a beer he might get Russ to relax. "I've got half an hour before the clinic opens. Wait a minute. I'll get my coat." But he'd taken no more than a step back into the inner office when Russ's voice stopped him.

"On second thought, maybe we'll make it another night. I think I'd like to talk with Dana." His eyes bore relentlessly into hers such that it was all she could do to keep from looking away in guilt. But she didn't want to look guilty. She didn't want to feel guilty, at least on the matter of something romantic existing between David and her. That was what Russ suspected. It was up to her to somehow set him straight.

"That might be the best idea," she murmured, not quite sure how she was going to explain things to him, only knowing she had to do something. "David," she turned back, as much for a smile of encouragement as anything else, "thanks again. I'll be in touch."

He gave her that smile, plus a wink in reminder of his positive feelings toward her racing, then reached out to touch Russ's arm. "Are you all right?" he asked quietly.

At first David wondered if Russ would stalk off without answering. Even his terse "I'm fine" was a relief, if a lie. He was very definitely bothered, his features taut, his expression grim. If that was indeed jealousy he'd seen in Russ's eyes, it was a very healthy first. But David knew not to prod just then. And he suspected that Dana would have better luck reaching him anyway. It was, after all, her race. Silently he wished her luck as the two disappeared from sight.

Russ held Dana's arm tightly as he ushered her outside to the parking lot and his car. "But mine's over there," she pointed out. "Why don't I follow—"

"I want you with me," he snapped. "You can get your car later."

She had the distinct feeling that she was in for an ordeal before she next saw the inside of her car. "Maybe we should . . . make it another time, Russ. I mean, you're angry—"

"You're damned right I'm angry!" he roared, then caught himself and quieted down. Reaching the car, he opened the passenger's side and stowed Dana securely before taking his place behind the steering wheel. Starting the engine, he headed from the parking lot without further word.

"Where are we going?" she asked as bravely as she could. She felt intimidated and unworthy.

"My place."

"I don't want—that's not a very good idea!" To her relief, there was a spark of fire in her yet. She'd been buoyant leaving David's office; Russ's mood had shattered all that. She assumed she had a right to be upset herself.

He shot her a cutting glance. "Why not?"

"Because . . ." Because it was *his* territory and, spark of fire or no, she had no wish to feel totally outclassed. "Because it's in the opposite direction from my house."

"And you're worried you won't get home in time to get that good night's sleep you need? Tell me, would you have waited for David to finish up at the clinic?"

"I was just leaving David's when you arrived."

"So you said," he muttered skeptically.

Dana looked at him then, struck by his forbidding tension. "You're wrong, Russ," she said softly. "You've jumped to a very wrong conclusion."

"Have I?" he asked, his hands white-knuckled on the steering wheel. He felt as though he were a fool of the first order. "Here I spent the entire day telling myself how stupid I've been, even going so far as to drop in on David in the hopes of nonchalantly discussing my feelings for you over a glass of beer, and I find I'm too late. You've already gotten to him." He took a sharp curve at unnecessary speed, realized his folly, and forced his foot up from the floor. "What is it about David that you find so fascinating? You were hooked on him the minute I introduced you. What is it, Dana? Why him and not me?"

For the first time she heard a twinge of hurt in his voice and she felt her own quagmire thickening. How simple it would be to tell him of her fascination with David—simple yet incredibly complex. As she wallowed in the dilemma, Russ went on.

"Wrong conclusion, you say? You meet the guy last night, ask constant questions about him all the way home from the restaurant, then bingo, walk out of his office arm in arm, no less. What other conclusion is there?"

"It wasn't arm in arm," she defended herself softly. "His arm was around my shoulder. For God's sake, he's a doctor. And you're right; he's too old for me. You tell me, Russ," she demanded, growing furious at the absurdity of his suspicion. "What *is* it about the man that could fascinate me?"

Russ didn't answer. His eyes never left the road. His profile was stony, his every muscle taut. Dana barely made out the pulse throbbing at his temple as he turned the car onto a private road that wound around and up and finally delivered them before a house that even at night was as large and impressive as its owner. But she had no time to sit in leisurely admiration. Brusquely helping her out, Russ took her elbow and herded her toward the door with an authority that suggested she might not have been able to find it herself.

She might not have. Her emotions were in a state of turmoil, her faculties for reasoning not much better. The events of the past twenty-four hours, from the moment Russ had picked her up at the library the night before, were so very different from all that had come before in her experience that she felt bewildered. The Dana Madison of old would never have been out with a man like Russ Ettinger, much less been reduced to complete abandonment in his arms. The Dana Madison of old would never have paid a visit to a sports doctor for the purpose of getting the okay to race. *Race?* Was she really serious?

Flipping on a single light, a soft, recessed one in the living room, Russ dropped his coat on the sofa en route to taking a stand before the fireplace with his back to Dana. Given the maelstrom of her thoughts and the dark cloud seeming to envelop Russ, she wanted to turn tail and run. Yet she was trapped— trapped not only by the physical isolation of their setting, but by the power of her own feelings.

It was the latter that took hold as she stood still, her eyes never leaving Russ, his tense back, his bowed head. She watched as his fist opened and closed on the mantel. In spite of his anger, she ached for him. She wanted to go forward, couldn't, felt all the more inadequate for her hesitation.

"Take off your coat," he growled, but his voice had mellowed. In place of that raw anger was an undercurrent of hurt. It bound her to him all the more.

Without argument she unbelted her coat and dropped it on a nearby chair. Then she stood, unable to sit, unable to move toward Russ. She didn't stop to examine her surroundings, simply kept her eyes on him, waiting.

After what seemed an interminable silence, he turned. His hair had fallen low on his brow, giving him an even more ominous look. But his expression was pure pain, and his voice, when he spoke, nearly broken.

"I've never felt this way, Dana. I've never wanted anyone as badly as I want you. I was up all night, trying to understand why I'd been so upset last night. Jealousy isn't usually my style."

She stood with bated breath, waiting for him to go on. One part of her was ecstatic. To think that he might feel as strongly—even love her—thrilled her beyond reason. To know that there was still a vital part of her he didn't know, though, terrified her. It might all be so perfect, if only there weren't this devastating secret she kept from him.

His eyes burned into her, seeking that depth he'd always known was there. "I'd planned everything so well, taking it slow, hoping to ease that fear of yours by gradually letting you come to know me, trying to build your frustration level until you simply couldn't resist."

"I can't," she whispered.

"Then why? Why another man?"

"There isn't another man. Not in that sense."

"That was what I told myself today. That it was all in my mind, an insane jealousy born solely of my need for you. Then I found you with David and . . . and . . ."

"There's nothing between David and me. He told you. It was a medical visit."

"A medical visit?" One brow jacked up. "But why? You're in perfect health. Why the intense interest in him last night? Why the sudden call on him today?" When she hesitated to answer, he moved forward, covering the distance between them until he stood directly before her. "Why, Dana? I need to know."

She bit her lip and looked up at him, feeling the pain of her own needing so badly that she thought she'd scream. She had to tell him, had to. But it was hard.

"I love you," he whispered, lifting a hand

to gently stroke her cheek. "Don't you know that by now? I thought to trap you with my clever plotting, but instead I'm the one who's been trapped."

Tears suddenly filled her eyes, blurring his image until all that remained were the sensual effects of him—the warmth of his hand, his manly scent, the vibrancy radiating from his body, the very evident pain he struggled to endure. Suddenly she didn't doubt that he loved her, and her own pain increased.

"You shouldn't love me," she cried. "I'm not right for you."

"Why not? Maybe if you tell me yourself, I can understand it. All I see now is a woman who is warm and giving, who is intelligent and dedicated, who could give me her mornings and evenings and nights if she would, who runs with me and accepts me, who would probably even massage my knee if I let her. I see a woman whose quiet life is the only kind I've ever wanted to share." He took a shuddering breath. "Why aren't you right for me? Tell me, Dana!"

"Because you . . . you don't know everything about me!" she whispered miserably, tears dripping unnoticed down her cheeks.

"Then tell me! Give me something to dislike! Damn it, Dana, I need to know!"

When she tried to lower her head to escape the intensity of his gaze, he refused. His hands held her there, so close, so gentle, yet relentless. She felt ugly and small and aching all over.

Seeing her anguish, Russ spoke softly. "I can't imagine anything about you not to love, though you've been down on yourself from the first. I keep wondering about that deep, dark secret you harbor. It's got to be the cause of the fear in your eyes, but I can't, for the sweet life of me, conceive of anything so horrible as to put a dent in the love I feel for you. If it's something in your past, some lurid affair—"

"It's not that!" Well, not really.

"Then what? Are you in love with someone else? Have you taken some vow of chastity? Is your life bound to some force that I don't know about?"

"No, no, no!"

"Then tell me, Dana! Why *were* you at David's today? It's that, isn't it? You're so open on every other point. It's something physical, isn't it?" She closed her eyes then, forcing an even greater torrent of tears past her lids. "Oh, baby, don't cry. . . ." Her quiet sobs were muffled against his sweater as Russ put his arms around her and held her tightly. "Don't cry. I don't think I can bear it!"

But she couldn't stem the tears, any more than she could speak to explain them. She loved Russ; he loved her. And she was positively terrified that what she was about to tell him—and she knew the time had come—would do something to change all that. For the first time she could understand the agony he suffered at not being able to ski. To have had something—even these few seconds of shared and declared love—made its loss all the more traumatic.

His hands stroking her back with such strength and care soothed her to the point that her tears slowed, then stopped. She held tight to him, her own arms wrapped fiercely around him, as if to savor these last moments of innocent bliss. It was Russ who set her back.

"Tell me. Please, Dana. I need to know, whatever it is," he pleaded.

She looked at him then with every bit of the love she felt and an awful dread, praying for strength and forgiveness. Her voice was little more than a whisper. "I'm an asthmatic."

It was out. Told. The air between them didn't stir. Nor did she breathe, other than to vent a few lingering sobs. Her stomach knotted, her limbs shook as she awaited his reaction.

EIGHT

What?" His voice held raw disbelief.

She knew it. Instant disillusionment. But it was done.

"I have asthma," she repeated herself in despair.

"And *that*'s your deep, dark secret?"

"Yes."

He took her by the shoulders as though he would shake her. But rather than anger or disgust in his eyes, there was utter amazement. "And that's what's been haunting you all these days—*asthma*?"

"Yes."

"My God, Dana!" he cried, hugging her so tightly she thought her ribs would snap. "I thought it was something serious!"

"But it is!" She wedged her hands up and

levered herself back. "I've suffered with it since childhood! It's shaped my entire life! I grew up thinking of myself as an invalid—at least, that's how I was always treated."

But he was laughing. "And here I'd begun to think you had something fatal."

"It was almost as bad as that for me," she argued, hurt by his seeming insensitivity. "As a child I was kept indoors all the time. I couldn't play with other children. I couldn't do anything strenuous. And it wasn't much better as a teenager. My mind had grown; my body had grown. Nothing else had changed."

"But it did change."

"Finally. When I reached the age of twenty-five, I realized that what my parents called a life was no life at all. That was when I rebelled."

As much as he wanted to hear her tale, Russ was more concerned with the present than the past. All humor suddenly vanished from his face. "Dana, do you love me?"

"I do, Russ," she whispered from the heart. "God help me, I do."

When he hugged her this time, she gave in to it, feeling his trembling and the spark of hope welling within her.

"Then why didn't you tell me you had

asthma at the start?" he asked against her hair. "That was the problem on the road that night, wasn't it?"

"Yes."

"Why didn't you tell me?"

Her own voice was muffled against his chest. "I wanted to, then I didn't. I've gotten it so well under control that most people I know now don't know about it. It's so nice to feel whole, to be able to face people without seeing their pity. And you—it was a dream to imagine a normal relationship with a man."

She felt his thumb at her chin and had no choice but to look up and meet his gaze. His tone was uneven. "Are you saying that you've never had a normal relationship with a man?"

Unable to face him with this final confession, she took advantage of the loosening of his arms to pull away and turn her back. Head bowed, arms wrapped tightly around her middle, she spoke timidly. "I tried once. It was after I'd made that break from my parents. I said to myself, You're twenty-five. It's about time you learn what it's all about. There was this fellow. I'd dated him several times." She shrugged. "I thought he'd be as good a teacher as any."

When she paused in search of strength, Russ coaxed her with a gentle hand on her neck. "What happened?"

A soft moan escaped in memory of the pain and she felt her eyes flood anew. "I, uh, I went to bed with him. Only we . . . we never really got started." She brushed at the tears with the back of her hand. "I had an . . . an attack. He was appalled." She shook her head and spoke as in a daze. "I've never seen such a look of disgust . . ." Then she caught in a sob. "I don't think I could bear seeing that on your face, Russ." Yielding to the agony she felt, she buried her face in her hands.

Russ was behind her then, his arms around her, his own voice filled with pain. "I'm sorry, so sorry that you had to live through that. Had it been me, I would never have let it happen." He rocked her gently, his breath warm by her ear. "He couldn't have come close to feeling what I feel for you. When we make love, it'll be beautiful. You'll see."

"Oh, Russ," she began, but her words gave way to silent weeping. When he turned her in his arms, she buried her face against him and held to him as though he were the last living thing on earth. "I'm so frightened. If anything should happen . . ."

"It won't," he crooned. "I won't let it." Prying her face from hiding, he turned it up to his. "I love you, Dana. That's all that matters."

"But if we were . . . and I had an . . ."

"Then I'd hold you until it passed and we'd start all over again. You can't get away from it *or* me. Now that I've got you, I'm not letting you go."

She saw it on his face, an undying but gentle determination. "And you'd love me . . . even knowing . . ."

His eyes glistened. "I'd love you even if it *were* a fatal disease, which, thank God, it's not." He shook his head, his gaze filled with admiration. "In fact, I think I love you all the more for your asthma. When I think of what you've done in spite of it . . ." His lips touched her cheeks, one then the other, to absorb her tears. Then his mouth moved to her eyes, her chin, her neck, kissing the anguish away. "You're beautiful, so soft and sweet-smelling," he murmured, taking her earlobe between his teeth and nipping gently.

She sucked in her breath. "And you really love me?" It seemed too good to be true, that knowing everything, he'd still think her woman enough for him.

"How can I prove it?" he asked, momentarily drawing his head back. "I know. I'll put it up on a billboard," he teased, raising his hand to shape the words. "Russ loves Dana. Better still, I'll have them write it in the sky for all the world to see."

"Russ!" she chided, blushing.

"But the best idea is this." He lowered his head and kissed her thoroughly, pressing her body against his, leaving her dizzy with desire. "Let me make love to you," he whispered against her lips, coming up for a ragged breath. "I want to show you how perfect it'll be for us. Then you'll know for sure."

Her arms remained tightly coiled about his neck, but he felt her stiffen. *"Now?"*

"Now." He caressed her with his voice.

"It's so . . . so sudden."

"You want me." He drew slow circles against the small of her back. "I can feel it in your body."

"I—I don't know. I'm frightened, Russ."

"But it's me, Dana. I'm with you. Let's put an end to that fear for all time."

Her body trembled at the thought. She wanted him more than she'd dreamed possible. The holding and kissing and words of love were only a prelude to something she'd pushed out of her mind as unattainable.

"Do you love me?" he asked, and she nodded. "Then trust me. I can make it right. *We* can make it right. It'll be a first for both of us."

She saw the smoldering light in his eyes, felt its kindling in her body. When he kissed her again, his lips parted hers and she sighed her surrender into his mouth. She loved him. She wanted him. This time it had to be right.

Taking her unsteady hand in his, he led her down a hall to his bedroom, where he released her only to put on a low light by the bed and draw the covers back. The cocoa brown sheets were warm and beckoning, two matching pillows fluffed and ready. Then Russ came back to take her in his arms and kiss her again while his hands began a slow exploration of her fragile curves.

"I love you," he whispered against her throat, then looked at her with such gentleness that her breath seemed stolen. "Trust me. Love me." His words warmed her. His lips, kissing her again, drove all thought of fear to the back of her mind. She responded with the force of her own desire, letting it transport her to a realm that made her momentarily oblivious to the work of his hands at her blouse. He released her lips to press moist kisses to their corners as he slipped the blouse from her shoulders, then let it drop with his gaze. "You're beautiful." His hands ran up and down her arms, his eyes delighting in the ivory sheen of her skin. Tingles of awareness surged through her, bringing a flush to her cheeks that was born as well of shyness. "So delicate and fresh . . ." he murmured as he lowered his head to kiss the swell of her breasts. His hands cupped their undersides, pressing them toward his lips. When her own natural swelling took over, he released the catch of her bra and gently peeled its lace away. The sight of her bare breasts was that of a treasure newly unveiled. He couldn't help but stare at her in wonder.

"Russ," she whispered as his gaze drew her nipples hard. "Please . . ." She wanted him to hold her, to touch her, to do something, anything, to ease both her unbidden modesty and her frustration.

"Wait," he gasped. Working hastily, he whipped his sweater over his head, then tore at the buttons of his shirt. When he too was bare from the waist up, he brought her back against him, enveloping her in his arms, helplessly arching his hips against hers. His groan was a vocalization of the rapture she felt as she raised her arms to the warm, hard muscles of his back. His skin was smooth and moist, its musky tang eminently masculine. Against her breasts the fine-haired texture of his chest created a heady friction. "See how well we fit?" he moaned, able for the moment only to press her closer, to try to make her irrevocably a part of him.

Dana felt parts of her coming alive that she hadn't known existed. Her skin seemed to catch the fire of his, her every pore open and ultra-sensitive to the impassioned heat of his body. She felt his hands on her back, covering every inch of her naked skin, sending a burst of awareness to her loins with the downward tracing of her spine.

She knew what was coming. She ached for it, though it frightened her. But something was so very right about it all, as though Russ were the half of her for which she'd spent her life waiting. It wasn't just the physical, she knew. Rather, he was the completion of her, the fulfilling of her destiny as a woman. He was the richness without which she knew she'd always be incomplete.

His hands were everywhere then, moving as if in slow motion, gently reassuring her every step of the way. Her skirt fell slowly to the floor, then her stockings. When she wore only her panties, she shivered in anticipation. Again she ached for him to hold her. But his hands were busy at her head, removing each pin, letting fall the wealth of blond hair that reflected as a deep, shimmering lambency in his eyes. When she thought her legs would give way, he lifted her into his arms and sank back onto the bed to cradle her. Her arms were around his neck, their faces a hair's breadth from each other.

"That first night on the road," he whispered, his softly urgent words binding her all the closer to him, "when I found you breathing so hard, I had a mad urge to protect you, to take care of you. I will, Dana. I swear it. Nothing can come between us now."

Protectiveness, emotional need, physical desire—he felt all these things plus a strange fear of his own at the thought of all he wanted to do with and for her. He was awed by the responsibility of her care, by the thought of what he was about to do to her even then.

But he loved her more than he'd ever loved another living thing, and he knew that without her his life would be as meaningless as the last few years had increasingly been. He ached for her in so many ways, not the least of which was his wish to overcome that initial fear of hers, to conquer the pain and set the glory free.

Bent on that path, he held her gently, his hands worshipping her body, savoring the smooth length of arms and legs that were as sleek and well-formed as that filly he'd calmed once before. When he kissed her deeply, his tongue primed her for those deeper thrusts to come. When she responded with rising desire, he knew she'd set herself in his care.

His hand grew bolder then, shaping her breasts to his fingers, rubbing the pad of his thumb back and forth over her nipple before skimming the silken flesh of her stomach to find the inner warmth of her thighs. She gasped once, then let him have his way, feeling the pleasure his fingers gave, finally arching against them in mindless need.

Laying her carefully down on the sheets, he quickly shed his clothes until, wearing only his briefs, he came back to her. "I've dreamed of having you here in my bed. Was I alone in the dreaming?"

"I haven't dared dream that," she came back from the heavy mist of arousal to whisper. "I was so frightened." It was true. Her first experience in bed with a man had been so traumatic that she hadn't wished ever to repeat the farce. But this was no farce, and there was nothing traumatic about it. She was breathing fast and free, aware and loving every nuance of his sensual assault, bothered only by a futile attempt to gauge his needs. "I want it to be good for you, Russ," she cried at last, "but I don't know what to do."

"Don't do anything, honey," he crooned in a voice deep and soothing. "Just relax and enjoy. Later you'll know what to do. Just do whatever feels good to you, love. Just like when you kissed me last night in the car." Remembering that particular fire, he ran the tip of his tongue along the curve of her mouth, coaxing it apart until her own tongue met it.

And so the ritual gained momentum, speeding onward with each caress. Russ touched her everywhere, gently, coaxingly. He stroked her shoulders, her hips, and her thighs before returning to caress her breasts, to palm their tips to even greater rigidity.

When she moaned at the impact of his riveting assault, he was fast to reassure her. "It's all right," he panted, struggling to control his own burgeoning desire. "Let it happen. It's all so glorious." And it was. She felt warm and sensuous, more than ready when his lips followed the trail of his hands to heighten the electricity to sizzling proportions.

The feelings inside were all so new. "I love you," she murmured, in need of justifying her vivid response to him.

"That's what makes it so special," he rasped. "It's the love we share that makes it beautiful." Finding the innocence of her mind boggling, he was nearly beyond that point himself. But he held his dire need in check, carefully keeping his lower body against the sheet so as not to frighten her with the evidence of his thorough arousal. His hands and mouth made her ready for him. She was fine, as he knew she would be.

Very cautiously he slipped his hand beneath the band of her panties. When she demurred, he gentled her again. "Don't be frightened. You're so soft there." His hand moved lower, invading slowly, rhythmically, as he waited for her response to resume at a higher level with each foray.

When he found her deepest warmth, she moaned. Again he crooned soft words of love and reassurance. As her passion mounted, his fingers delved farther, finding her erotically moist. "You're so ready for me, so right," he whispered, probing deeper.

"Russ!" she cried.

"It's beautiful." His mouth covered hers then and, self-consciousness overpowered by a greater force, she arched helplessly against his hand, straining toward that something new and wild and wonderful he promised.

Pausing only to strip off his briefs, Russ eased her panties down her legs. He nearly lost control then, seeing her fully naked on his bed. He felt awed by her natural beauty, overwhelmed once again by the weight of responsibility. She was precious and trusting. He wanted everything to be so right this first time.

Beginning all over again, he kissed and touched and teased her until at last she cried out in sweet torment, "I don't think I can bear much more . . ." Her body was suffused with a crimson flame. She felt consumed from the inside out.

Only then did he move over her, positioning himself, twining his fingers through hers and holding them by her head. She looked up into his eyes, seeing their adoration, adoring in turn the strength of his features, the rich darkness of his hair, the looming power of his shoulders. Then his head lowered and she closed her eyes to bask in his confidence.

"I love you, Dana," he whispered, then covered her lips as, with uncompromising purpose, he thrust forward. When she cried out softly into his mouth, he eased the pressure of his lips to repeat "I love you" over and over again in agonized refrain. He might have been the virgin for the pain he felt.

He was very still then, moaning softly, "There. You're mine for all time." And he looked down at her with tender fear. "Have I hurt you too much?"

"Yes . . . no . . . oh, Russ, I feel so . . . fulfilled."

His eyes smiled his joy. "Filled, not yet fulfilled. We'll go slow."

He tried. His initial strokes were cautious and measured, accustoming her to the feel of him moving inside her, tenderly paving the way for the more ardent thrusts his body craved. But conscious pacing became wishful thinking with Dana slowly coming to life beneath him. As discomfort gave way to newness, which in turn gave way to the first ripples of pleasure, she felt things she'd never even dreamed of. There was a liquid excitement, a searing thrill, a quickening, a yearning for more.

Instinct dictated her movement as he'd said it would. Her body met his with greater force. Their breathing came faster. He thrust deeper. Their bodies grew slick in the heat of passion.

Dana reeled in delight, stunned by the pleasure she felt, both the fire within and the beauty without. Her hands couldn't touch him enough, surging over the broad expanse of his back, feeling it arch, then bow with each lunge. She had no idea what she could have ever feared. The only shortness of breath was born of passion; the only fear was in the mind-shattering heights to which he carried her.

She was burning ever hotter, as though a glowing coil down deep within her was fast reaching the point of explosion. With abandon she strained higher, arching against him in search of the final wonder of which her body was aware before she was herself. When she cried out his name, he sensed her bewilderment.

"It's good, honey. Let it come."

It came in a blinding explosion that seemed to shake her body endlessly, its aftershocks nearly indistinguishable from his own shuddering release. Only after what seemed an eternity of mindless bliss, he collapsed on top of her, their bodies mutually spent.

Fearful of hurting her any more than he had, he slid to the side, leaving an arm beneath her breasts, a leg between hers. Though his limbs continued to tremble, he propped himself on an elbow, needing to see her face, to know her reaction. What he saw assuaged whatever fears he might have held. Her face was flushed, her eyes luminous, her lips soft, love-rouged, and smiling.

"Breathless?" he gasped.

"Um-hmm."

"Me, too. I love you very much."

"Me, too." Then, finding a spurt of strength from a mysterious source that had to embody love and relief and a whole other world of rapture, she threw her arms around his neck. When he fell back to the bed, she came over half atop him. "Oh, Russ. Thank you."

He hugged her, then settled her in the crook of his shoulder. "You were wonderful," he said. "Do you have any idea how unique that was?"

"Having never done it before," she teased, "no."

He easily reached to her bottom and gave her a playful pinch. "That wasn't what I meant at all." Then his voice grew soft in awe. "For a woman . . . the first time . . . not to mention reaching that together."

Understanding, she nestled all the closer to his chest, studying it for the first time, threading her hands through the damp mat of hair she found there. "It was beautiful. You're beautiful." Her eyes wandered lower. "Thank you," she whispered again. "I'd been so afraid all these years."

"Yet you're fine. I told you. We're right for each other. Neither asthma, nor anything else, can detract from what we have."

"You love me?" She couldn't hear it enough.

He smiled, understanding. "I love you."

Emboldened by the afterglow of their lovemaking, she let her hand wander where her eyes had roamed. "Your body is so different from mine. So strong and firm."

He recalled the way she'd moved so fiercely against him in the throes of passion. "I wouldn't exactly call you a weakling, my love. Not that I'd want you muscle-bound and hairy like me." His hand glided over the smooth skin of her hip. "It's your softness that turns me on so. Your softness and sweetness and the depth of your feeling."

Basking in his love, she gave a sigh of pleasure. To know that she'd been able to please him was heady knowledge indeed. Her fingers found his hip bone, traced it, then slid to rest in the smooth adjoining hollow. "I love you," she whispered in time with the beat of his heart.

They lay quietly together then, savoring the ecstasy they'd shared. As their pulse rates steadied, Dana grew aware of her naked, love-warmed flesh against his. The thought brought a new tingling. To her amazement, when she thought herself totally sated, she felt that tingle shimmer through her body with a slow, seductive curl. Her hand moved again, secretively creeping across his chest, inching lower as a tender yearning was reborn and grew. With sweet aching she pressed closer. When she heard the sharp intake of his breath, she tipped back her head in bewilderment.

Russ knew what she was doing, even if she didn't. "Not again tonight, honey." His expression held the tenderness that his raspy voice lacked. "You'll be too sore inside." His lips twitched at the corners. Then he paused and whispered, "Love me?"

"I do," she murmured, and nestled against him. "I've never been as happy in my life."

"Marry me?"

Her head shot back up, her blue eyes glimmering. He'd chosen the one reply in the world that could have possibly added to her happiness. *"Really?"*

"Of course really," he drawled. "When a man has waited as long as I have to ask that of a woman, he's not about to joke. *Really.*" Playfulness retreated as he looked at her. "Will you marry me, Dana?"

"Oh, yes," she breathed, beaming from ear to ear.

"God, I can't stand this!"

"What?"

"You're crying again."

She laughed through the tears and pushed them away with her fingers. "I can't help it," she sniffled. "I'm so happy."

"Does that mean you'll be crying for the next fifty years?"

"No, no. I'll get used to it someday."

"When?"

"When will I get used to it?"

"When will you marry me? We can take out a license on Monday and be married by the end of the week."

She hesitated, only then recalling the earlier events of the evening and those other plans she had for the future. "June?" she ventured meekly.

"June? I can't wait until June! A February bride is every bit as beautiful. Just think, a honeymoon in the Caribbean sun, lying on the beach, making love on a balcony overlooking waters as blue as your eyes."

"You are a romantic," she teased, then propped herself on an elbow and grew more quiet. "I want to wait, Russ. There's something I've got to do first."

"What?" He had no time to waste words when it came to something that mattered so very much to him.

She took a deep breath. "I have some running to do. I want to race."

"You what?"

"I want to race." She repeated it quickly, unsure as to whether he was disbelieving or, worse, disapproving. "I've decided to do it. That was what I saw David about today."

He held up a hand. "Wait a minute. I don't understand. I thought you were the non-competitive type. You never spoke of racing before."

"I never wanted to do it before."

"Why now?"

"Because I need to do it now." Her eyes held the haunted cast he knew all too well.

"But why?" He felt suddenly concerned, knowing now of her condition.

She studied her fingers mingling with the rich pelt of hair on his chest. "I guess I have to prove something to myself."

"But you've done so much already. Even fun running must have been a challenge."

"It was." Her lips curved ruefully. "It took ages to work up to a mile, let alone five."

"Then why go further? And why race?" His thoughts were of the pressure of competition. He feared her trying. He feared her failure.

When she raised her eyes to his, though, he saw her determination. "Because I think I can do it. And so does David. I have to prove something."

"Not to me."

"To me. If I can do this, I can do anything. Don't you see?" she pleaded with a soft urging that held him spell-bound. "I want to be good for you, Russ. I want to be a wife who can give you everything you ask. I want to know that if we *do* marry, I'm . . . fit for you."

"Oh, Dana," he murmured, his tone filled with love, "you're fit for me just the way you are. I don't want Wonder Woman. I want you."

Her smiled was tinged with sadness. "I couldn't be Wonder Woman if I tried. But there are times when I feel so inadequate and restrained. I'm sure it's a legacy of my childhood"—she grimaced and corrected herself—"of my adulthood, for that matter. You—you're so much more. You've done so much more. If I can do this, I might be able to see myself in your class."

"To hell with my class!" he exploded. "It's nothing!"

If anything, his vehemence made her all

the more firm. "Not to me. I saw your ad for ski boots in that magazine. And my guess is that you've got a stack of trophies around here somewhere."

"Damn!"

"No, Russ. It's wonderful, all of it! I want you to be proud of them *and* me. I want to be proud of myself!"

He was quiet, his eyes dark. He recalled how she'd been on the road that night, cold and frightened, struggling for air. When he spoke, his voice was deep and dangerously low. "I won't let you do it, Dana. If anything should happen . . . I *can't* let you do it."

Pushing off from his chest, she sat up abruptly. She was oblivious to her nakedness, oblivious to his. "It's not your choice to make. It's mine!" Her eyes flashed fire. "I spent twenty-five years of my life doing what others told me to do. More accurately, not doing what they told me not to do. When I couldn't stand it anymore, I broke away. It was an effort, Russ, going out on my own. I was unsure of everything, and scared to death. But I made it. And I'm not about to give up that feeling of freedom." She softened her tone to a beseechful one. "Please believe me. I'm not so bull-headed that I'd do something stupid. That's why I was so curious about David last night, why I called him first thing this morning, why I told him everything and asked for his advice. It'll all be slow and careful. And if I can't handle it, I'll stop." Her voice grew tremulous. "I love you. But I won't be an invalid again. I want your love, your companionship, your protection, but not your smothering. At least not where my asthma is concerned."

It seemed forever that, jaws clenched, Russ stared at her. The love he felt was overwhelming, as was the need to keep Dana healthy and sound. It was all part of the responsibility he had so readily assumed. But he heard her words and the need they expressed. Finally he shook his head in defeat. "I don't know whether to throttle you or to hug you." Stretching one long arm up, he opted for the latter. He pulled her back to his chest and enveloped her in a fierce embrace. "You have my love. You'll always have that. And my companionship and protection and respect." He paused, then sighed. "As for my smothering, you'll have to help me there. The thought of anything harming you ties me in knots."

His warmth seeped into her and she slowly relaxed against him again. "Nothing will harm me if I have your support. You do understand what I want to do, don't you?"

Begrudgingly, he did. "I understand that you've got this"—he wanted to say bizarre, but restrained himself—"this image of what you want to be. And one part of me adores your determination. The other part . . ."

She held her breath. "Yes?"

"The other part despises myself for having brought you to it."

"Despises? Come on, Russ. Where's your sense of optimism?" Then for the first time she grew unsure. Her pleading gaze met his. "Do you think I can do it?"

The question, in its deepest implication, symbolized the crux of the matter. She wanted, she needed his approval. Much as she was determined to run the race herself, she needed Russ to make it all worthwhile.

"You can do it!" He gave her a squeeze. "I do believe you can do anything you set your mind to." Then, with a remembered thread, he frowned down at her. "But why June? We can be married within the week and you can do your racing as Dana Ettinger."

When she shook her head, blond silk

shimmered over his chest. "As beautiful as that name sounds, it's the other, it's Dana Madison who's got to prove something to herself. And the race I really want to run is at the end of May."

"The end of May?" he echoed meekly. He had the uncomfortable feeling that he'd heard her right. Though he'd never taken to racing himself, he was involved enough in the local sports community to know what was coming up. "Dana, you're not planning . . ." But he clearly saw that she was. Her quiet words only confirmed it.

"I am. The Maine Coast Marathon. It's the ultimate challenge."

"It's suicide!" He reared up over her, pushing her back down to the bed. "Do you know how long runners train for a marathon?"

The reverence with which he said it only enhanced the prospect. "No," she answered boldly, "but I'll find out. If it's a matter of endurance, I'll run every day and build up slowly. You can run with me. It'll be fun."

"Hah! I can't run that distance," he grumbled. "At least someone here is aware of his limits."

His glower brought a wholly new thought

to Dana's mind. How would he take it, competitor that he was, if she went the distance? Would he be jealous? Feel belittled? She'd heard of the emotional problems some men had when their wives earned more money than they did, yet she couldn't believe Russ's ego to be so fragile. Indeed, he had accepted his limits, if reluctantly.

"Would . . . would it bother you if I did?" she asked fearfully.

"Hell, no! That's not the point! The point is that a marathon is grueling work. The marathoner subjects himself to side stitches and shin splints and blisters and muscle cramps, not to mention the wall. You hit the wall and you're running on fumes."

"Very heady ones," she injected purposefully. She, too, knew a little of the experience. Even turning the pages of articles on racing, certain phrases had jumped out from beneath the pictures of exuberant athletes. "You're forgetting about the high of it all, the sense of euphoria, the joy of crossing that finish line."

Deflated by the gleam of anticipation in her eyes, he let out a long breath. She was right. His years of athletic competition, though not in road running, had familiarized him all too well with the sweet smell of success.

"No," he mused, "I can't forget that. It is something to experience."

"Well, I want to experience it. Just once. To know what it's like and be able to remember it as you do." She raised her hand to the face that had become so dear to her. His cheek was pleasantly rough along the shadow of his beard. "Will it upset you?" she asked again, needing to hear him say it in a calmer, more reasonable tone of voice.

He pondered her concern for a moment before smiling his resignation and shaking his head. "No, honey. It won't upset me in that sense. I'm not thrilled at the thought of you putting yourself though that torture. But you're determined, aren't you?"

She nodded. "Will you help me? I can't do it without you."

"You mean you'll need someone to rub you down when those muscles begin to rebel."

"Hmm," she murmured, innocently seductive. "Not a bad idea."

At the sign of his smile she glowed. When she reached up to him he took her into his arms without question, knowing he'd help her find her way through hell if that was where she chose to lead him. His hands slid across the smooth skin of her back, settling at opposite sides of her waist. "Dear heart, I love you!"

She let her head fall back and savored his fiercely tender expression. "Then why are you growling?"

"Growling?" He feigned innocence. "That wasn't me. That was my stomach. I'm hungry."

It was the first Dana had thought of supper. She'd been planning to stop at the market after seeing David. It seemed ages ago. "I'd say I'll cook you something, but my refrigerator's nearly as bare as I am." A healthy flush crept to her cheeks. "I could use something, too."

"Feeling weak?" he asked with a wicked grin that sent ripples of excitement through her.

"Not weak," she returned, smiling coyly. "Tired, perhaps, but very satisfied."

He ran a strong forefinger along the line of her lips, felt them part, then reluctantly dragged his hand away. "How about if we get cleaned up and then go out for something? There's a steak place about ten minutes from here."

"Sounds good."

He gave her a quick kiss on the nose and rolled from the bed. "You stay here."

"Where are you going?"

She watched as, in all his naked glory, he marched toward the bathroom. His limbs were long, athletic, and very, very masculine. "You'll see. Don't move."

She didn't, other than to reach down to pull the sheet over her. Not that she was cold; the heat of their love, enhanced by the sight of Russ's lean, muscular physique, precluded that. Yet it was still all so new. She felt called upon to exhibit some semblance of modesty.

It was a token gesture. Russ returned moments later to whip the sheet from her and sweep her into his arms. "What are you doing?" she cried, clinging to his neck. Within seconds she was being lowered into an oversize whirlpool bath. "Russ? Ahh. This is *beautiful!*"

"Thought you'd like it." He grinned at her delight. "Sorry that I don't have any bubbles for you, but I'm not stocked for women. You're the first whose pretty bottom has ever touched my porcelain."

Her pleasure was doubled. "This'll do," she purred. The warm water swirled about her sore limbs. Luxuriating in it, she closed her eyes and stretched, then realized the amount of extra space and glanced shyly up. "Are you coming in?"

"Me?" Feeling a tightening in his groin, he cleared his throat. "Uh, no. Not tonight. I'll take the shower. Cold." With that he stepped into the nearby stall, closed the door behind him, and put the water on full force. He had a lot to think about, not the least of which was getting his hands on David Ahearn.

NINE

Why in hell did you encourage her?" he demanded when, after brooding in the waiting room for twenty minutes until the doctor's Saturday morning emergencies were settled, he entered the inner office shortly before noon.

Knowing precisely what he was talking about, David stood his ground. "Because I think she can do it. I examined her. She's in excellent health."

"She's a chronic asthmatic!"

"She did tell you then."

"Last night. And that she planned to race. And that she's set her heart on the Maine Coast Marathon."

"The marathon?" That was news to him, though he was neither terribly surprised nor particularly disturbed. "Well, I suppose if she trains properly . . ."

"David, it's crazy!" Russ bellowed. "I mean, okay. If she wants to do a three-miler or a ten K, that's fine. She could probably go either of those distances now without killing herself. But a marathon? That's insane."

"Ambitious, perhaps. But not insane."

"Come off it, David!" He stalked to the window in disgust, then turned back with a vengeance, his hands hooked low on his hips. "Sure, she could train for it and get her hopes way up there. Then what happens if she collapses with muscle cramps halfway through? What happens if, God forbid, she has an attack? Forget the physical part of it all. Do you have any idea what that could do to her spirit?"

Sitting behind his desk, David was miraculously calm, the epitome of the level-headed physician. "I have some idea," he said. "Don't forget, I've been dealing with athletes and their problems since you hooked me on it, my friend. There have been ones who've made it and ones who haven't. It's a question of weighing and balancing things."

"What things?" His dark brows lowered farther. "Life and death? Success and failure?

Glory and despair? You're into playing God now?"

Beginning to see that Dana wasn't the only one smitten, David was gentle in his chiding. "It was her decision, Russ. She was the one who sought me out. She was the one who came with the express intention of racing."

"But you could have discouraged her."

"In good conscience, I couldn't have. There's no valid reason why she shouldn't try to race, given the shape she's in and what she's already doing. Personally, I'd rather have her run with my supervision than without. As it is, I've warned her to take it slow." He paused to study his friend. "Perhaps I can be more objective about her condition than you, Russ. I'm not the one who's in love with her."

Russ stared at him in anguish before sinking wearily into a chair. After dropping Dana at her house and leaving her with a lingering kiss and a promise to pick her up the following afternoon, he'd spent most of the night torn between the joy of love and the agony of worry. "I don't want anything to happen to her, David," he said, his expression now more grim than angry. "She feels she's got to prove something to herself. She won't marry me unless she does it. What if she can't do it? What then?"

"Then it'll be up to us to convince her that what she *has* done is the real accomplishment. She's a sensible woman, Russ. Sure, she may be stubborn on this score. But considering where she's come from, it's understandable."

Russ dropped his head back and closed his eyes. His brow remained furrowed by thoughts of all that he'd learned the night before. When he returned to David, it was with a loud sigh. "And you think that medically she could do it?"

"With that will of hers, she's got a good chance."

"But *medically*? *Can* an asthmatic run that far?"

"It's been done before. Listen, I told Dana that I'm going to consult with two respiratory specialists next week. I'll get to it on Monday. In the meantime, I'll tell you everything I know about her condition in exchange for lunch. Fair?"

They spent an hour and a half at it, after which, only marginally appeased, Russ spent the afternoon poring over the books David suggested he read.

Dana, meanwhile, pored through the volumes on racing and marathoning that she'd rushed out to purchase that morning. Between her ensuing excitement and the heady awareness of her love, she was fairly floating by the time Russ arrived. She opened her door to find him wearing slim-fitting jeans, a heavy white turtleneck sweater that set off his dark good looks to perfection, and a down vest of rich royal blue. Taken momentarily aback by the magnificence of his build and the fact that this man could truly love her, she stood tongue-tied and shy.

"Well?" he prompted her, breaking into a grin and opening his arms. It was all the invitation she needed. She was in his arms then, clinging to him, returning his kisses with a slow, burning fire. Suddenly they were in her bedroom, their clothes strewn hither and yon, their naked bodies reacquainting themselves with barely leashed desire. Russ couldn't get enough of her lips, her firm, high breasts, the gentle curve of her hips and bottom, her deeper warmth in that lower region. She, in turn, reveled in his manliness, in the muscularity of his shoulders, the breadth of his chest with its soft mat of hair, in the firmness of his torso, the leanness of his hips. She touched him where she'd never touched him before and found his urgent moans to be as heady as his instant physical response. Between words of love and sighs of delight, their bodies merged in magical frenzy, building to a shattering climax that left them breathless and spent and all the more in love.

Dinner was no less dreamlike, nor was the night they spent together. It was only when they ran the following morning that they discussed Dana's plans.

"I'll take it slow, Russ. I promise. I've got it plotted out. There's a five-mile race in Boston next month, and a 10K up here in April. On Mother's Day there's an eight-and-a-half-mile run on Martha's Vineyard, then the Coast Marathon at the end of the month. It's perfect. Step by step."

Measuring his pace to hers, he stared down at her. "You've been busy."

"I have to be," she responded excitedly. "There's not that much time."

"You could wait a year, you know. Start with several of the smaller and mid-length races this year, then shoot for the MCM a year from May."

"And wait till a year from June to be married?" She knew just how to shut him up.

He grunted and sprinted ahead, slowing only when he'd gotten rein on his frustration. "You win. But on three conditions. You'll have to let me pace you. You'll have to keep in close touch with David. And you'll have to agree that if it becomes too much, you'll stop."

"Then," she exclaimed, "I can do it?"

It took a while, but his nod finally came. Vaulting into him, she threw her arms around his neck. They came to an abrupt halt on the side of the road.

"Thank you, Russ!"

He savored the feel of her slim body against his, then growled in her ear, "You would have done it anyway, wouldn't you?"

"Probably." But she wasn't at all sure. She half suspected that if she'd had to choose between racing and Russ, she'd have forsaken all thought of the former, despite the toll it might have taken on her. "I love you so much!"

A low groan came from the back of his throat as he pressed her closer. "Come spring, know what I'm going to do?" She shook her head. "In the middle of a run one day, I'm going to drag you off into the tall grass by the side of the road and make love to you there and then. See what you're in for?"

She pulled back to slant him a mischievous smile. "I'm not complaining, am I?"

With a fast-sucked-in breath, he gave her a firm slap on the bottom. "Now, let's run."

They did. Every morning henceforth. Russ all but moved in with her, spending most every night in rapturous reward for any hours of daytime separation. Together they mapped out a plan for her training. When the formal okay came from David at the end of the week, it all went into effect.

Dana was exuberant, in love, and feeling stronger than she ever had in her life. It was noticeable in the perpetual flush on her cheeks and the very feminine sparkle in her eyes. Though Liz saw far less of her than usual, she shared Dana's excitement about Russ, as did those few other of her friends in whom she confided. To her parents she said little, simply, when they asked why there had been no answer on her phone for two successive evenings, that she was dating someone. They prodded, as she'd known they would, but she was determined to keep Russ to herself until she had proven what she'd set out to prove. If, for some reason, she failed, the less they knew of it the better. In such an eventuality, the last thing she'd need would be an "I told you so."

Reminding herself that their concern stemmed from love, she felt more than a little guilty. But she wasn't ready to introduce Russ to them, and was particularly fearful of having him see her through their overprotective eyes. He'd been hesitant enough about her racing from the start, without needing additional voices on the side of restraint. At least David was on her side. For that she was infinitely grateful. As for her parents, she looked forward to being able to tell them everything in time.

According to schedule, she began to slowly increase her distances the next week. Russ ran with her every day, sometimes in the morning from her place, sometimes in the evening from his. They savored their privacy, spending every free minute together, learning everything there was to know about the other as their love deepened. In quiet times they talked, in more impassioned times they made love. If Dana was astounded by the extent of her hunger for him and the utter abandonment with which she came to life in his arms, she was ever rewarded by Russ's genuine delight. She ran, she worked, she loved. She felt on top of the world, unable to imagine anything setting her back. But it was a high that was destined to be tarnished when, one Sunday evening, after they'd spent a blissful weekend at his place, reality made a stark return.

Russ turned his car from the main road to find her drive crowded with cars, not the least conspicuous of which belonged to the police.

"My God, what happened?" Dana cried, sitting rigidly forward.

Russ forced his voice to remain calm. "Relax, honey. We'll see." He brought the car to rest at the nearest available space, then jumped from it and caught her arm as she ran forward.

"That's my parents' car! And my brother's! And the police? Why are the police here?" Breathlessly making her way through the front door with Russ close beside her,

Dana stood staring aghast at the gathering that seemed divided into no less than three separate huddles. "Mother! Dad! What's the matter?"

It was her father who saw her first. "Dana!" At his cry, the rest of the crowd looked up. All conversation ended, leaving the atmosphere one of abruptly suspended frenzy. "Dana! Thank God!" Separating himself from his group, he was by her side instantly. Her mother was close behind.

"We've been frantic, Dana! *Where have you been?*"

"I've been with Russ," she answered, looking in bewilderment from one face to the other of the strangers in her living room. "But I don't understand. What's happened?"

"Russ?" Her mother eyed him dubiously. "This is the man you're dating?"

"That's right, Mother. Russ Ettinger . . . my parents." She'd hoped the introduction to have been made under more propitious circumstances. After all, these were her parents, and this was the man with whom she'd be spending the rest of her life. But she was totally distracted. "What's going on?"

Her brother stepped from the side to take her shoulders. "We've been worried sick about you, Dana. When Mom and Dad couldn't get through on the phone, they imagined something terrible had happened. Then, when they came over and found your car sitting outside an empty house . . ."

With the first inkling of understanding, Dana's stomach jumped as though she had taken a low blow. "You mean . . . all this . . ." She looked around. Aside from her parents and Max there were two uniformed policemen and a neighbor. "All this because I wasn't here?"

"Are you all right, baby?" her father said, placing a custodial arm about her shoulder and drawing her farther from Russ.

Though Russ, like Dana, was dumbfounded at what they'd stumbled into, he was eminently aware of the distance being put between Dana and him. Stepping forward, he spoke with confidence.

"She's fine, Mr. Madison. She's been with me all weekend."

He might not have said a word. Ignoring him, Dana's father spoke to her in hushed tones. "It's all right. You can tell us anything."

"Tell you anything?" She stopped dead in her tracks. "What are you talking about?"

Her mother took up position by her other

arm. "If he used any force to get you to go with him, you needn't be afraid to say. We've got the authorities right here."

Appalled by their insinuations she wrenched her arms from her parents' grip and took a step back. Her heart pounded; her fists were clenched. Turning to the police, she gritted out, "Thank you for coming, but you can leave now. As you see, my parents have made a terrible mistake." Her parents had called in the police when they'd found her gone. She was mortified.

Russ, too, was dismayed. "That's right, gentlemen." He managed to speak more calmly than Dana had. "There's no problem other than a family misunderstanding. If you'll excuse us now, we can straighten things out."

"Sure thing, Mr. Ettinger," one of the cadre of men said, stepping forward and motioning his fellows to follow.

"Wait! You can't let him go—" Dana's mother began, only to be stopped by her husband, who not only sensed the command in Russ's voice but had heard the respectful tone with which he'd been called by name. She turned questioningly. "Jim, you can't let them leave! Something's got to be wrong here. Dana would never go off for the weekend with a man—"

"Mother!" Dana cried. She'd never been as humiliated in her life. "That's enough! This is insulting!"

"But you wouldn't do that."

There was a pathetic look of hurt on her mother's face, but Dana was too emotionally wrought to see it. Her whole body trembled. "I'll be thirty years old next week! I'm a big girl now! I don't have to check in with you."

"But your asthma—"

"*My asthma has nothing to do with this!*" she screamed, furious and breathing hard. Russ put an arm around her shoulder in an attempt to calm her, but she continued to lash out. "I'm a grown woman and in love with this man. If I want to spend the night or the weekend or the month with him, *I will.* And I don't need your permission!" She barely saw the movement of figures toward the door as the gathering broke up. Her anger was directed solely at her mother, but tears blurred her image. "You had no right to do this!"

"Dana," Russ murmured softly, squeezing her shoulder, "take it easy. We'll talk it out."

But she was thoroughly distraught. "They

had no right to humiliate me . . . or you this way! Are those cops really supposed to think you'd abduct a woman and keep her against her will for the weekend?"

Max spoke up then, the counselor at his most conciliatory. "It was a mistake, Dana. Mother and Dad were worried. We were all worried. You may be right, that you're a grown woman. But your life has been different. And you could have let us know."

She turned on him in anger. "Do you let them know every time you leave your house?"

"It's different with me."

"It's not! I'm no different!" she gasped, but she knew she was. She could feel it in her chest, that telltale tightening. "It's you all who've made me different!" Her gaze widened to encompass her parents as well. "You've made a spectacle of me!" she panted, laboring with each breath. "You've ruined it all!"

Miserable with the knowledge of what had happened and the effect it was having on her, she broke away. "Leave! Please!" Running from the room, she escaped to her bedroom and slammed the door loudly behind. Bursting into tears, she sought refuge in a fan-back wicker chair, huddling in its corner, tucking her knees up, burying her face against the cool denim of her jeans with her hair falling forward as a shield against the world. In her anguish it took her several seconds to separate sobs from wheezing. When the awful sound of the latter penetrated her web of unhappiness, she stumbled to the dresser, inhaled deeply of her medication, then tripped back to the chair.

Her abrupt departure left everyone in the living room staring. Her mother made a move to go after her, but Russ was a step ahead. He held up his hand. "Please, Mrs. Madison. Let me talk with her." His tone was polite yet firm, its stilling effect reaching the older woman this time. When he saw her take a step back, he proceeded, passing down the short hall, quietly opening Dana's door. At first he couldn't find her; the room was dim. Then the sound of wheezing came to him and, seized by sheer and sudden terror, he ran toward it.

"My God!" he whispered, crouching down before her. He'd thought her upset but hadn't imagined this!

"Tell them . . . to leave!" she gasped, her

face buried deep. "Get them . . . out of here! I can't breathe when . . . they're here!"

He reached out to stroke her hair, to draw it back from her face. "What can I do, Dana? Have you taken anything?"

She nodded. "I just did. Make them go!"

"Look at me," he whispered urgently, then took her face in his large hands and forced it up. It was ravaged with tears and frighteningly pale. His own color drained completely. "Are you all right?" He would have gladly rushed her to the nearest hospital, but was held back by saner thoughts. The attack would pass. Dana knew how to handle it. Moreover, she needed to do it herself.

"No," she wailed, crying harder. Between that effort and the more urgent one to breathe, she felt dizzy, weak, and defeated. With her parents and brother present, she was an asthmatic through and through. Only with them gone would she be able to pull herself together. "It was all so perfect . . . until they . . . get rid of them, Russ, please?"

At her pleading note, he bolted up and made for the door, gathering his composure and slowing his step only when he reached the living room arch. Three heads turned his way, each pair of eyes as wary and concerned as the next.

"Is she all right?" Jim Madison stepped forward, his voice cool.

"She'll be fine," Russ prayed aloud. "But maybe it would be better if you folks left us alone."

Dana's mother stared, aghast. "Left you alone? We're her parents. It's our place to be with her. None of this would have happened if you hadn't—"

"Excuse me, Mrs. Madison," Russ interrupted as kindly as he could, given the urgency he felt to return to Dana, "but you're wrong. It is my place to be with her now. I love her. Come June, she'll be my wife. She's my responsibility, and I believe I'm capable of taking care of her."

"She's sick, isn't she?" her mother railed. "I heard it just now. She can't hide it from me."

"Look," Russ returned, "she'll be fine." He could feel himself breaking into a cold sweat, wanting to be with Dana, not here. "She's taken her medicine and I'm going in to sit with her." He stared at three worried faces and conceded that their hearts were in the right place. "If you want to stay for a while, have a seat. When she quiets down, I'll let you know." Inviting no response, he turned on his heel and retraced his steps to the bedroom. When the door was once more firmly shut, he quickly crossed the room and hunkered down by Dana's knees. Her head was against the back of the chair, her eyes closed. The pitiful rise and fall of her chest tore at his gut.

"Dana?" he whispered, frightened and unsure. He raised a hand to her pale cheek. "How is it?"

As she squeezed her eyes shut, tears trickled down her cheeks. "I didn't want . . . you to see this."

"I'd have had to see it sometime or other." His voice was incredibly soft. "It's not so bad. What can I do?"

The rattle of her breath was nearly as loud as her words. "My medicine. On the dresser. I'll take more."

He had the inhalator instantly in hand. "Can you do that—take a second dose?"

She nodded, relieving him of the small bottle and setting aside self-consciousness to breathe deeply of the mist. As soon as she was done, Russ took the bottle from her.

"What now?" he asked. Her pallor terrified him.

"We wait," she gasped, breaking into another sob.

"Oh, honey," he moaned, aching for her, "it's all right. Here"—he took her into his arms—"come sit with me." Shifting to the bed, he propped himself against its headboard and secured her in the circle of his arms. He held her gently, fearful of further hindering her breathing. "There," he crooned, stroking her hair, "you'll be fine."

"I'm sorry, Russ."

"Don't be a goose."

"You don't . . . deserve this."

"You're right. I keep asking myself the same question, how a time-worn bachelor like me deserves as wonderful a woman as you."

She nudged him with her shoulder. "You know what I mean! My asthma."

"Shh. Keep still and it'll get better." He tucked a long strand of flaxen hair behind her ear and kissed the top of her head. "Shh." With the gentle rocking motion of his body, he felt her taut muscles begin to relax. He lightly massaged her back, whispering soft words of encouragement, trying desperately to control the runaway beat of his heart so that she wouldn't know the extent of his fear. He'd never seen this before. Briefly he wondered what would have happened had he not known she had asthma. He thanked heaven she'd told him, and that he'd taken so much time since to learn about the affliction. At least he knew that he shouldn't panic yet.

Tipping his head to the side, he looked down at her face. Was it wishful thinking, or was her color better, the wheezing eased? "How're ya doin'?"

Her voice, though weak and very soft, was clearer than it had been. "Not bad."

"You sound better."

"It's working."

"The medicine?"

"You."

"That's my girl!" He dared hug her more tightly. "When her sense of humor's back, I know she's on the mend."

They sat quietly for a long time until very gradually Dana's breathing returned to normal.

"There. That passed pretty quickly."

"Um-hmm. It usually does."

"How do you feel?"

"Tired. A little shaky."

"That's to be expected."

"And angry and embarrassed and—"

"Whoa! Give it time, Dana. Let yourself recover first, then we'll cope with the rest." Her words, though, were a reminder that her parents were probably still in the other room. Very gently he disengaged himself, laid her back down on the bed, and drew the quilt over her.

"Where are you going?" she asked in alarm, missing his warmth in spite of the quilt.

"The living room. I'll be right back. Just rest."

When he turned to leave, she reached out. "Russ? I love you," she whispered, feeling it never more so than at that moment.

He came back to sit for a minute longer on the edge of her bed. Leaning down, he touched his lips to hers. It was a kiss kept gentle by his concern for her physical state, yet it held his answering words of love. Then, with a parting peck on her brow, he straightened.

"Stay put. I'll be back." He walked to the door and shut it firmly behind, praying that she wouldn't hear conversation, should her parents still be in the house.

They were. Max appeared to have left,

but the elder Madisons were ensconced on the sofa. At his appearance they came to their feet. Concern was etched on their faces, wariness remained well in evidence.

"How is she?" Diane Madison asked.

"She's doing fine. The worst seems to have passed."

"You know that she's prone to this, don't you? The last thing she should have done was to have spent the weekend away from here."

Though Russ's tone was kind, he didn't yield. "The weekend she spent with me had nothing to do with this flare-up."

"The . . . excitement. It's not good for her."

"The excitement was wonderful." Russ recalled it well. His expression mellowed at the thought of the love it embodied. "No, what brought on this attack was returning here to find things in an uproar. Dana is convinced that you have no faith in her ability to function as a healthy individual. When she's with you, she sees herself as you see her, first and foremost an asthmatic."

"But she has been that all her life," Jim pointed out, coming to his wife's defense. "We've always had to protect her."

"But she doesn't want to be protected. She doesn't need to be protected. For the first time now, she feels like a normal human being. She's independent and active and almost entirely free of her asthma. Tonight was a setback for her. But she'll rebound."

"You're very confident in your knowledge of our daughter, Mr. Ettinger," Jim said with one eyebrow cocked. "How long have you known her?"

"Since the first of January."

"But she didn't tell us about you," Diane argued, hurt once more. "Not until very recently."

Sympathizing with a mother's emotion, Russ tried to speak gently. "Maybe she was afraid that you'd do exactly what you have done—that you'd tell her it wasn't healthy, that she couldn't handle it. But it *is* healthy, Mrs. Madison. It's the healthiest thing in the world. And I think she's happier than she's ever been. I know I am."

"You do love her?" Jim asked, giving Russ his first glimmer of support.

"Very much. Too much, I fear at times. My natural instinct is to protect her, much as you folks did for years. But there's a fine line between protection and overprotection. I've got to watch myself. Dana doesn't need to be coddled. It could do more harm than good." Afraid of pushing his luck and eager to return to Dana once more, he forced a tentative smile. "Listen, I can imagine that you're both exhausted, though I really think we should talk more. Will you be our guests for dinner on Friday night? Dana could get back to you with the details."

"That would be nice," her father said before his wife could object. Not that she would have. She was wavering. But Jim Madison wasn't taking any chances. He, for one, wanted to learn more about Russ Ettinger. And, as it was, they saw Dana all too infrequently. He'd look forward to it.

"You did *what*?" Dana shot up in bed when Russ returned with the news.

"I invited them to have dinner with us on Friday night."

"Russ! How could you?" But even before he answered, she saw how pleased he was with himself.

Standing beside the bed, he seemed all the taller and more commanding. "It's the best thing I could have done. They love you dearly. What happened today was caused by that. And," he chided her gently, "there is valid argument that you should have let them know you'd be gone. Given the past—not that it's right—they felt they had reason to worry." When Dana gave a snort and looked away in annoyance, he sat down on the bed before her. "It's a two-way street, honey. If you want them to accept you as you are now, you've got to let them know you as you are now. It seems there's been a stalemate, culminating in tonight's fiasco. They see you as the dependent little girl; totally rejecting that, you shut them out of your very independent adult life. We've got to meet them halfway. Dinner might be a start."

"I don't know, Russ," she protested, discouraged. "You've seen firsthand what they do to me."

"These attacks are emotionally induced. You love them—or you wouldn't be so bothered." His point was well taken.

"I suppose." She reached for his fingers.

"Let's try, Dana. My parents are dead, or I'd want you to know them. Let me get to know yours."

With his earnest expression she realized how very highly he prized family life. She'd already sensed it with Sondra and Danielle, both of whom she'd instantly liked. Perhaps, after all, she'd feel the same if, God forbid, something happened to her own parents.

"You'll . . . you'll be on my side, won't you?"

"Always!"

Friday night's dinner went beautifully. To Dana's astonishment, the initial tension faded quickly, yielding to a relatively relaxed, even enjoyable evening. Russ must have been right, she decided. Her parents had responded to her meeting them halfway. And, to her delight, she'd made it through without the slightest shortness of breath, aside from that which Russ induced, much later when they were alone, with his love-making.

All that remained to make her happiness complete was running the marathon.

TEN

As they ran through March and April, both Russ's knee and Dana's lungs behaved gloriously. According to plan, Dana slowly built up her endurance until she could run seven, eight, then ten miles at a stretch. Her growing sense of power compensated for any fatigue she felt. Also as planned, she entered and ran the shorter races, overcoming an initial nervousness to finish in fine form. Russ's presence helped. Though she was concerned about his knee, she found solace in the knowledge that the pace he kept beside her was slower than what he might have kept had he been racing on his own. He was a source of comfort and encouragement. For, determination or no, she did have lingering doubts as to whether she could actually make it. With Russ by her side she felt stronger than ever.

The arrival of May brought not only pale green buds to the trees and the gayest of the wildflowers to the roadside fields, but the successful completion of her first fifteen-mile run . . . and a slow mounting tension. It was a time of extremes, from the high of being with Russ, of adoring him to distraction, of envisioning the fast-approaching day when they'd marry to the low of fearing that somewhere along that twenty-six-mile stretch she'd falter, and fail.

Russ too thought of the future and fell victim to that overprotective urge to which he'd been susceptible from the start. As the days passed, his worry grew. Even Dana's regular contact with David did little to ease his concern. With each blister or side stitch, he wanted to beg her to stop, to pamper her, to dote on her, to save her from further discomfort and risk. But he knew it wasn't what she wanted or needed and, though continually torn, he restrained himself.

Their days fell into a pleasant pattern. They awoke at six to run in the early morning warmth, breakfasted together, then went their separate ways until reunited after work.

Though Russ should have been freer, with the ski school closed for the season, an increase in business at the store, plus another opening, took up the slack. At night both were usually exhausted. Their favorite evenings were early ones, spent quietly with dinner and the soft conversation of lovers. Mindful of earlier vows, they did make a point to visit with Dana's parents again, as well as to spend time with Sondra and Danielle. Danielle, in particular, seemed to idolize Dana, standing in awe of what she attempted to do with her running. Russ couldn't have been more pleased.

The weekends were divine, filled with love and each other. And running. Since Dana's training schedule demanded longer treks on Saturdays and Sundays and therefore tired her more, their other plans were geared toward relaxation. Once they drove north to the lake region and rented a cabin for the night. The two days they spent on Martha's Vineyard combined running with other adventures in ecstasy. One hazy Saturday in mid-May they journeyed to Kennebunk to study the marathon route, then stayed on for lobster dinners overlooking the water in the late-afternoon mist.

And then there was the time, as Russ had promised, that they made love in the dewy grass at dawn. Regardless of what came after, Dana would always remember that morning. The air had been warm from the start, even before the horizon had grown pale, then slowly golden. Having run six miles, they'd reached a particularly deserted spot where tall grasses and thick stands of trees corded the road and stretched back into God's country.

When Russ suddenly took her hand, she looked up at him in surprise.

"What?"

"Come on." Veering sharply, he drew her through the thigh-high grass down a shallow incline.

"Where are you taking me?" she shrieked in delight.

"To the woods," he growled.

"Russ!"

"Shh. You'll wake the wildlife and they'll all be watching."

She knew that roguish gleam in his eye far too well to mistake his intent. "But we can't, Russ. Not in public."

There was nothing public about the spot where he finally stopped, a luxuriantly fresh grove of trees forming a rich green cocoon around its sun-streaked center. "It's our land as well as theirs," he reasoned, turning her into his arms.

"But I'm all sweaty!" she whispered, though even then tingling inside. In essence, their earthiness and the sweet smell of spring blended erotically.

"I love you this way," he groaned against her neck, tonguing that moistness, then following it up with warm kisses strung from the hollow of her throat to her jaw and her chin. By the time he arrived at her lips, they were parted and waiting.

There was little need for preliminaries. As he devoured her mouth, then sucked greedily on her tongue, he lowered her to their mossy bed and stretched his body over hers. His hands ranged over her breasts, finding their peaks a magnetic force from which only the raging fire in his loins drew him. His ardent fingers clamored downward over her stomach to her thighs as her own relished the flexing muscles of his back, the lean hardness of his waist, the firmness of his buttocks. Their skimpy running clothes, a sensual conductor at first, quickly became a hindrance to what both urgently wanted.

With fervent "I love yous" rasped against her lips, Russ dragged her shorts over her thighs to her knees. Levering himself only high enough to shove down his own shorts, he surged back upon her and entered her in with one fluid thrust.

"Ahhhh, Russ!"

Her exclamation of raw pleasure brought a low animal sound from his throat. "You're always ready. So warm. Soft but tight and exciting." As that very tightness enveloped him, his breath caught and he could say no more.

There, in the stillness of the forest on a damp cushion of moss, Dana experienced a joy that defied description. She felt him move within her, stroking, then plunging deeper. Her hips rose to meet his, receded, then rose again. Her nails dug into the sinewed swell of his back, urging his total absorption into the haven of her femininity. When at last their bodies erupted into the furthest reaches of fulfillment, their cries broke the silence of the morning to imprint the sound of love upon the world.

Breathlessly they clung together, reluctant to part. It was only when the cry of the wild geese overhead reminded them of the traveling they had yet to do themselves that Russ finally slid to her side.

"Beautiful?" he asked, adoring her with his eyes.

"Beautiful," she gasped, beaming. "There's only one problem."

"Problem? What's that?"

"How are we going to get home?"

His gaze swept over her naked lower torso, lingering at the juncture of her legs until she crossed them saucily. "We're somehow going to have to manage to pull on our shorts."

"That's not the point. My legs feel like rubber."

"Rubber?" He slid his hands over the limbs in question, gently massaging as he went. "There. Any better?"

She gave a provocative whisper. "Some."

"Damn it, if we lie here much longer I won't be able to get my shorts on at all." As Dana laughed brightly, he struggled into his shorts, then leaned over to tug hers back in place. "There. Good as new."

"Almost. But you wrecked my training for the day."

He arched a wicked brow. "Depends what

you're training for, slow-twitch." Standing, he gave her a hand up. "Come on. I'm hungry."

"You're always hungry," she mused in coy delight. His only answer was the possessive arm he draped across her shoulders as they slowly returned to the road.

That morning was, in effect, the start of Dana's countdown. With two weeks to go until the marathon, the anticipation began to mount. Running eight miles a day, plus another twelve or fifteen on the weekends, she felt strong and optimistic. With plans for one twenty-mile run on the weekend before the race, she hoped she'd be ready, as did Russ.

But she was tense, wondering, as the time neared, whether indeed she'd find the twenty-six-mile stretch that little bit too much. She could read all there was to read about marathoning without knowing a thing until she'd tried it herself.

Though outwardly confident and every bit as encouraging as he could be, Russ was concerned as well. He wondered how her lungs would take that final exertion, those last six miles that she'd never done before.

David checked her out weekly, assuring him that she was physically sound. But Russ's concern was even more for the emotional. He feared what might happen if, by some chance, she had to quit early. She'd poured so much of herself into the effort; he dreaded seeing her fail.

During that last week they spent many a night quietly in each other's arms, making love with words and closeness alone. They discussed the route of the race and a strategy for running it as they waited for sleep to overtake them. Invariably it was Russ who lay awake long after Dana's breathing had grown slow and rhythmic against his chest.

All too soon Saturday arrived. Packing overnight bags bearing running clothes, Vaseline, Ben-Gay, bandages, and sun block, they drove to Kennebunk to go over the course a final time, get their racing numbers, maps, and information on water stops and bathroom and medical facilities. Dana had long since given up trying to convince Russ not to race with her. In spite of her concern for his knee, she saw that he was adamant. And she wanted him there. It never occurred to her that his presence would detract from what she as an individual was trying to do.

After all, he couldn't run the race for her. But if he was there by her side when she crossed the finish line, the victory would be shared, and therefore all the more sweet.

Sunday morning dawned warm but overcast, an ideal day from Dana's point of view. Rising with the day's first light, she and Russ left their motel room to join the other runners shortly after six for the seven o'clock start at the high school. There was an excitement in the air that she hadn't experienced in any of the other races she'd run. But then, she'd never run the marathon. It was different, special, the race of races if the throng of 998 other avid runners was any indicator.

Stretching and warming up on the high school lawn after they'd checked in, Dana diverted her thoughts from fears for herself to fears for Russ. He seemed tense. He assured her he was fine. But she wondered.

The minutes seemed to crawl. They took long drinks of water. They jogged in slow circles. They waited. Dana's pulse had already jumped the gun, racing full force as the crowd slowly moved toward the starting line. Struck once more by insecurity, she felt out of place among the other runners. But Russ was always with her, talking softly, bolstering her, instructing her to take long, deep breaths to relax herself. David approached them once, offering water and encouragement. Though she knew that he was there in an official capacity, on call for any of the runners who ran into trouble, she felt a special pleasure in his presence. Over the months he'd become a good friend as well as an advisor. She needed all the support she could get.

With ten minutes to go, her stomach began to jump. Russ put his arm around her shoulder and calmly talked to her. With five minutes to go, her fingers grew cold. He took them in his and warmed them easily. With two minutes to go, she had dire second thoughts, all revolving around her love for Russ, her need to make him proud, her need to make herself proud. There was so very much at stake. Her whole body quaked as she took her position.

Then they were off. There was no turning back. Of the thousand runners gathered, she seemed the lone one who didn't check a watch. Her goal was to finish. That was all.

The pack moved slowly at first, gradually thinning as each runner found his pace. With the adrenaline flowing free, the first five

miles were exhilarating. The danger, if anything, was in breaking out too fast; the real
effort was toward self-restraint, toward running the race evenly, toward precluding early
exhaustion. Previous worries and tension
receded in deference to a preoccupation
with deep breathing and a steady stride.
Dana and Russ ran side by side, mindless of
those others who sped on ahead, as unaware
of others who fell behind. Their concentration was intense, focused solely on the road
immediately ahead. Though they exchanged
an occasional smile, few words were spoken.

With several more miles behind them,
they reached the ocean. For many who'd
come distances to run, it was the beauty of
this particular marathon. The pounding surf
was a beat to run to, the image of the waves
as refreshing as the cool, clear water offered
by race aides to be quickly gulped then
splashed over faces, heads, throats. For
many runners the ocean was a distraction.
For Dana it was a source of strength. She
knew it. She loved it. In its everlasting ebb
and flow, it represented the steady breathing
for which she strived.

Moving inland once more, they crossed
the river and passed through Dock Square.

Though closed this early in the morning, its shops were quaint and as cheerful as those locals who'd chosen the spot to root the runners on.

Ten miles into the race they returned to the oceanside. Feeling herself beginning to tire, Dana dutifully drank the water that Russ passed to her, smiled gratefully at him, then turned her thoughts inward once more. The last thing she wanted to do was to think of how far she had yet to go. Rather her mind honed in on her breathing; so far, she was doing fine.

Kennebunkport's roads undulated gently, the strain of the rolling hillside offset by the enthusiasm of the spectators. This, too, was different from the races she'd run in the past. Awareness of the trial of the marathoner made the onlookers' appreciation all the more heartfelt.

Cape Porpoise was glorious, the New England shore encapsulated. With the pungent smell of the fish shacks filling her nostrils, Dana knew that the halfway point was behind her. She felt momentarily buoyed, ignoring the blister forming on her heel, the sweat pouring down her neck, the chafing of her thighs where she hadn't smeared enough

Vaseline. The faint ache in the muscles of her legs were nothing, though, compared to the high she felt. She'd long since gotten her second wind and her third, and she was breathing freely. Freely.

Then Russ faltered. It was seventeen miles into the race and they were wending their way inland again.

"What is it?" she cried, catching the awkward tilt of his gait.

"My knee." As it was, he had an Ace bandage around it for support. Evidently that wasn't enough.

"Bad?"

"We'll see."

After another mile, with another water station appearing in the distance, he spoke again.

"I'm stopping up ahead, honey."

"To rest?"

"For good."

"You can't, Russ! We're almost there!" Several runners passed them as they slowed their pace.

Russ's hair lay in wet strands on his forehead, sticking stubbornly to his skin when he shook his head. "This is it for me. You're doing great!"

"But I don't want to go on without you," she gasped, feeling suddenly unsure and frightened. "I can't!"

He moved closer as they ran, speaking firmly. "You can and you will. This is your race, Dana. It was all along. You're trained for it. You're psyched for it. And you're going to show yourself once and for all that you can do it."

The water stop was a hundred yards ahead, the distance closing fast. "But Russ—"

"No but's." He was limping badly, his eyes glued to hers. "Do it for me, love. More importantly, do it for yourself."

It was, indeed, what she needed to do, what she had to do. She knew it as he said it. Further argument was futile. "Oh, Russ, I so wanted us to do it together."

"There's a world of other things we'll do together. This . . . this is something you've got to do alone."

She should have been tipped off by the conviction in his voice, but her emotions were in far too much of a turmoil to ponder his words. "Will you be all right?"

He nodded and cocked his head toward the flock of attendants at the station. "I'll get you some water, then hitch a ride to the finish line." His gaze softened. "I'll be waiting for you there. Don't be long."

"Russ . . ." Her eyes filled with tears and a knot formed in her throat such that she was barely able to sip the water he grabbed from the sideline to hand her.

"Just remember to keep drinking. And relax. Breathe deeply. Pace yourself. Don't push. I love you, Dana. Keep that in mind." Taking her hand in his, he squeezed it tightly once, then dropped back. As though in slow motion, their fingers lingered, sliding against each other until only their tips touched. Then they parted as her preprogrammed legs carried her on. He smiled and waved, then threw a kiss and yelled it again. "I love you!" He cared little that the spectators cheered; his thoughts were solely on the woman growing smaller by the minute. She embodied his life and soul; he prayed she'd find joy at day's end.

With a twist of the road she was out of sight. Walking straight and strong, without the slightest limp, he let his pride in her carry him to the roadside where he waited for his lift to the finish line.

It took Dana far longer to recover. Brushing the tears from her face, she struggled to return her concentration to the race. But she was heartsick at having had to leave Russ behind, only then realizing how dependent she'd been on him. But dependence wasn't what she wanted. It wasn't why she'd ventured the marathon in the first place.

Having momentarily lost the evenness of her stride, she felt the start of a cramp in her leg. Then she thought of Russ and willed it away. He wanted her to finish; she would. She wanted to finish; she would. The thought of the glory at race's end gave relief to her aching limbs. With a rebirth of determination, she forged ahead.

When she hit Goose Rocks Beach, the wind was strong. For the little it slowed her, it was undeniably refreshing. Though the sun had yet to break through the thin cloud layer, its heat had had no such trouble. The air, as the route stretched inward, was a warm seventy degrees. Given the exertion, her body was far hotter. She reached for the water held out to her, then focused every sense on her running. In her periphery was the applause of the spectators. Their words of encouragement, coupled with her own tenacity, carried her toward the twenty-mile mark.

Once passed, she was on new ground. She'd never before run this distance, and though the force of momentum kept her stride steady, her legs had begun to cry out in rebellion. Not, however, her lungs; her breathing was well measured. She knew she could put up with most other woes, as long as her air pipes stayed clear.

Feeling alone without Russ, she found comfort in both the presence of nearby runners and the eager faces by the sides of the road. Crossing the line into Biddeford, she pushed harder to maintain her pace.

"You're doin' fine, Number 625!" a voice from the side yelled as she rounded the turn to parallel the ocean at Fortune Rocks.

"Keep it up, Dana!" shrieked another.

Daring to take her eyes from the road and glance to the side, she saw Sondra and Danielle, cheering and waving. She hadn't wanted them to come, she'd told Russ. The part of her that feared failure had exerted itself, so she thought. Yet now the sight of them brought a burst of adrenaline, a high that overspread her weariness to give her a much-needed pick-up. Smiling her appreciation, she passed them and ran on, her legs seeming to work automatically, driven by sheer will alone.

Leaving the ocean and heading inland for the last time, she knew that the end was in sight. Less than two miles. That was all. Her spirits soared higher. She had no idea how long she'd been running; time held only one meaning for her. It was no longer a question of whether she'd finish, but rather how soon she could be in Russ's arms again.

At the twenty-five-mile mark, she took a last gulp of water. Though her body felt drained of every bit of strength, she was riding a wave of exultation. The crowds grew, as did the din of their cheers. The excitement gave her the push that her body could no longer.

Then, as if in a dream, the finish line came into sight, and with it an emotional surge that was nearly her undoing. Concentration on running became a thing of the past; her sole focus was on reaching Russ.

Squinting against the brightening haze, she scanned the distant figures for a sign of that one for which she craved. But there were too many faces and her gaze blurred. She caught her breath, then tried to steady it, but it seemed useless. Her body was slick with sweat and ached all over. Not a single muscle seemed untouched by the cruel pounding she'd inflicted upon herself. Even her neck felt raw where her high ponytail had steadily thrashed her skin.

She brushed a stray hair away from her eyes and again searched for Russ. Where was he? The faces drew nearer. Her legs seemed made of jelly. Gritting her teeth, she willed herself on. She searched more frantically. If anything had happened to him . . .

Then she saw him directly ahead, just over the finish line, and her heart gave a thunderous hammer. He was there, waving her excitedly on, his face alight with joy and pride. He was all right. So was she. They'd make it after all!

She didn't even recall crossing the finish line, only throwing herself into Russ's waiting arms, laughing and crying at the same time. "I made it, Russ!" she sobbed. "I made it!"

"Of course, you did," he managed hoarsely, his own throat tight with emotion. Then, with a strong arm across her back to hold her up, he walked her aimlessly around to keep her muscles from cramping. He never thought to complain about the fingers that dug into his waist. They were amazingly strong, as was she. And he thanked God for it.

"Everything hurts so much, but it's so wonderful!" she cried. Tears of happiness streamed down her face, but she could think of neither where she'd come from nor what she'd done, only where she was right then. "I can't believe it!"

Then, shouting ecstatically, Sondra and Danielle bounded up and took their turns hugging her soundly. David followed within minutes to assure himself of her flushed features and clear breathing before wrapping her in his arms and swinging her in a victorious circle with an enthusiasm that probably would have lost him his license had the medical overseers been on guard. But Dana was unaware of any messages of discomfort that her roadworn body may have sent. She was numbed to everything but the delirium of the moment.

When she was finally back on her feet, she swayed toward Russ again. Then she stopped. "Your knee?" She studied it, then him. He was standing tall, showing no signs of pain. Indeed, he'd been walking her around without any trouble at all. "Your knee!" she exclaimed, suddenly suspicious.

"It's all right."

His sheepish expression gave him away.

"It is all right, isn't it," she stated, only slowly realizing the extent of what he'd done. He'd purposely dropped out of the race to give her that added sense of victory, that ultimate sense of pride. He'd had enough confidence in her. He loved her that much.

Dissolving into tears once more, she collapsed against him and coiled her arms about his neck. "Oh, Russ," she sobbed, "I love you so."

He crushed her to him, his voice shaky as he murmured against her hair, "No more than I do you, Dana. No more. But wait! I almost forgot." Gathering his composure, he set her gently back and dug into his shorts.

"Russ!" Dana stage-whispered, feigning embarrassment as she looked through her haze of tears at the others around them. "Not here!"

"Yes, here. You have a trophy coming."

"Trophy? But I didn't win!" She couldn't see the smiles of anticipation on the faces behind her. Her sights were solely on Russ.

"Oh, you won all right," he went on boldly. "Me." With that audacious announcement, he took her left hand in his and carefully slipped on the ring that still held his body's warmth.

"Russ!" she whispered, her breath stolen

by the incredibly beautiful marquise diamond on her finger. Its sparkle was made all the more brilliant by the tears in her eyes.

All else faded then, as she looked up at him. The sights and sounds of the finish line might not have been. Even those others who had come to matter so to her in the past weeks and months—Sondra, Danielle, David with his case of Perrier waiting to toast the happy couple—fell off to the side.

There was only she and Russ and the happiness they shared. For everything she'd experienced on this day, there was nothing to compare to the euphoria of their love. With her heart's message indelibly inscribed on her glowing features, she flowed into Russ's waiting embrace, knowing that, in finding him, she'd found herself at last.

In hardcover for the first time from William Morrow,

a powerful and unforgettable story of a woman's

search for her past from the renowned

New York Times bestselling author

Barbara Delinsky.

The Passions of Chelsea Kane

Available now

Please turn the page for a preview

From the plush comfort of the velvet love seat that had been brought into the library for the occasion, Chelsea Kane studied the blond-haired, blue-eyed, beak-nosed members of her mother's family and decided that wherever she was from herself, it had to be better stock than this. She detested the arrogance and greed she saw before her. With Abby barely cold in her grave, they had been fighting over who would get what.

As for Chelsea, all she wanted was Abby. But Abby was gone.

Bowing her head, she listened to the whisper of the January wind, the hiss of a Mahler murmur, the snap of her father's pocket watch, the rustle of papers on the desk. In time she focused on the carpet. It was an Aubusson, elegantly subtle in pale blues and browns. "This carpet is your father," Abby had always declared in her inimitably buoyant British way, and indeed Kevin was elegantly subtle. Whether he loved the carpet as Abby had remained to be seen. Things like that were hard to tell with him. He wasn't an outwardly demonstrative man. Even now, when Chelsea raised her eyes to his face in search of comfort, she found none. His expression was as heartrendingly somber as the dark suit he wore. Though he shared the love seat with her, he was distanced by his own grief. It had been that way since Abby's death five days before.

Chelsea wanted to slide closer and take his hand; but she didn't dare. She was a trespasser on the landscape of his grief. He might welcome her, or he might not. Empty as she was feeling, she couldn't risk the rejection.

Finally ready, Graham Fritts, Abby's attorney and the executor of her estate, raised the first of his papers. "The following are the last wishes of Abigail Mahler Kane . . ."

Chelsea let the words pass her by. They were a grim reminder of what was all too raw, an extension of the elegantly carved coffin, the minister's well-meaning words, and the dozens of yellow roses that should have been poignantly beautiful but were simply and dreadfully sad. Chelsea hadn't wanted the will read so soon, but Graham had succumbed to the pressure of the Mahlers, who had come to

Baltimore from great distances for the funeral and didn't want to have to come again. Kevin hadn't argued. He rarely took on the clan. It wasn't that he was weak; he was an eminently capable person. But where he championed select causes at work, there his store of fire ended, rendering him nonconfrontational at home.

Abby had understood that. She had been as compassionate as compassionate ever was, Chelsea realized, and let her thoughts drift. She remembered Abby bathing her in Epsom salts when she had chicken pox, ordering gallons of Chelsea's favorite black cherry ice cream when the braces went on her teeth, excitedly sending copies to all their friends when a drawing of Chelsea's won first prize in a local art show, scolding her when she double-pierced her ears.

More recently, when Abby's system had started to deteriorate, as was typical of long-term polio victims, the tables had been turned, with Chelsea doing the bathing, doting, praising, and scolding, and she had been grateful for the opportunity. Abby had given her so much. To be able to give something back was a gift, particularly knowing, as increasingly they both had, that Abby's time was short.

" . . . this house and the one in Newport I bequeath to my husband, Kevin Kane, along with . . ."

Houses, cars, stocks, and bonds, Kevin

didn't need any of those things. He was a successful neurosurgeon, drawing a top salary from the hospital and augmenting it with a lucrative private practice. He had been the one to provide for Chelsea's everyday needs, and he had insisted that it be that way. Abby had taken care of the extras.

Often over the years, Chelsea had wished she hadn't, for it had only fostered resentment among the clan. Abby's brothers and sisters had felt it wrong that a Mahler trust should be established for Chelsea, who had no Mahler blood. But Abby had been insistent that Chelsea, as her daughter, was to be treated like every other Mahler grandchild. So she had been, technically at least. She had a trust in her name that provided her with sufficient interest to live quite nicely even if she chose never to work.

". . . to my daughter, Chelsea Kane, I leave . . ."

Chelsea was an architect. At thirty-six she was one of three partners in a firm that was landing plum jobs up and down the East Coast. Moreover, she had personally invested in a well-chosen few of those projects, which meant that her profits were compounded. She lived quite nicely on what she earned.

For that reason, perhaps, the accumulation of assets had never been of great interest to her, which was why she barely listened to what Graham read. She didn't want to inherit

anything from her mother, didn't want to acknowledge that the woman was dead. Her
aunts and uncles didn't seem to have that
problem. Trying to look blasé, they sat with
their blond heads straight and their hands
folded with artful nonchalance in their laps.
Only the tension around those pointy noses
and their ever-alert blue eyes betrayed them.

". . . to my brother Malcolm Mahler, I
leave . . ."

Malcolm got the yacht, Michael the Packard,
Elizabeth the two Thoroughbreds, Anne the
Aspen condo. Still they waited while Graham
read on.

"As for the rubies . . ."

The rubies. Only then did it occur to Chelsea
that that was what her aunts and uncles had
been waiting for, not that any of them lacked
for jewels—or yachts, or cars, or horses—but
the rubies were special. Even Chelsea, who
would never dream of wearing anything as
showy, could appreciate their value. They had
been in the Mahler family for six generations,
traditionally passed from the oldest daughter
to her oldest daughter.

Abby had been the oldest daughter, and
Chelsea was her only child. But Chelsea was
adopted.

"I have given more thought to this matter
than to any other," Graham read, "and have
decided to bequeath the rubies as follows—my
sister Elizabeth is to receive the earrings, my

sister Anne the bracelet, and my daughter, Chelsea, the ring."

Elizabeth came out of her chair. "No, that's wrong. If the oldest daughter doesn't have a daughter, the entire set goes to the second oldest daughter. I'm the second oldest daughter."

Similarly appalled, Anne uncrossed her legs. "The pieces can't be divided. They were meant to be kept together. Whatever did Abby have in mind?"

"She must have been confused," Malcolm decided by way of polite invalidation.

"Or she was influenced by someone else," Michael suggested by way of benign accusation.

"A Mahler would never divide up that set," Elizabeth insisted. "The whole thing should be coming to me."

Kevin stirred then, not much more than a shifting on his seat, but, given his prior immobility, enough to draw attention. In a voice that was gritty with grief but surprisingly firm, he said, "The whole set should have gone to Chelsea. She is the oldest daughter of the oldest daughter."

"She isn't Abby's daughter," Elizabeth argued, "not in the real sense, not in the sense of having our genes and being able to pass them on. Besides, look at her. She's a career woman, She won't have a child. Even if she *was* of our blood . . ."

Chelsea rose quietly and slipped out the

door. She had no stomach for Elizabeth's words. More than any of them, she was haunted by the fact that she had no Mahler blood. For years she'd been trying to find out whose she did have, but Kevin had refused to discuss it, and Abby had been too frail to be pestered. So the issue had floated. Abby had been her mother in every sense that mattered. With her death Chelsea felt a sense of loss, a sense of coming unhinged, of losing one's anchor.

Abby had loved her. Physical limitations notwithstanding, she had doted on her to the point of near suffocation. Many a time Chelsea had wanted to tell her to buzz off. But Abby was too kind for that, and Chelsea wouldn't have hurt her for the world. She had fallen into a good thing when she'd been adopted. The Kane house was a haven. Love made it a secure, happy place.

Nonetheless she had been curious. She had wanted to know why she had been adopted, why Abby couldn't have babies of her own, how she had been picked. She wanted to know where she had been born, who her birth parents were, and why they had given her up.

Abby had explained, with a gentle care that Chelsea remembered even so many years after the fact, that her paralysis had made having children impossible for her, but that she and Kevin had badly wanted a child at the same time that a baby girl badly needed a home.

The adoption had been private and closed. Abby claimed to know nothing, and Kevin agreed. "You're a Kane," he insisted even when Chelsea was at her most outlandish. "It doesn't matter where you come from, as long as you know who you are now."

Chelsea drew herself up before the gilt-edged mirror that hung over the console in the hall. She was as tall and slender as any of the Mahlers and as finely dressed, but that was where the similarities ended. She had green eyes to their blue, and her long hair was auburn, with the natural wave that the a Mahler women envied only when waves were in style. Thanks to a motorcycle accident when she was seventeen that had resulted in a broken nose and subsequent surgery, Chelsea's previously turned-up nose was small and straight. Likewise, thanks to a dental appliance that she had worn as a preteen, the chin that would have otherwise receded had been coaxed into perfect alignment with the rest of her features.

She was an attractive woman. To deny it would have been an exercise in false modesty, and Chelsea was too forthright for that. She had come a long way from the unruly waist-length hair, kohl-lined eyes, and ragtag flower child look she had espoused as a teenager. Abby had been proud of the woman she'd become.

Now Abby was gone, and her family was in

the library bickering over a set of jewels. Chelsea was sickened. Had it not been for Kevin, she would have walked out of the house. But she didn't want to leave him alone. He was crushed. After anticipating Abby's death for so many years, he was finding the actuality of it hard to accept. Chelsea could fault him for thick headedness on the matter of her adoption, but not for his absolute and unqualified love for Abby.

The library door opened to Elizabeth and Anne. "We'll fight, you know," Elizabeth warned Chelsea as she strode past.

Anne pulled their furs from the closet. "The ring should remain in the family."

Without another word—not the slightest gesture of consolation, encouragement, or farewell—they left.

The front door had barely shut when Malcolm and Michael emerged from the library.

Chelsea handed them their coats.

Silently they put them on. Malcolm was fitting his hat to his head when he said, "You made out quite well, Chelsea."

She stood away with her hands by her sides. "I'm afraid I wasn't paying attention to the details." They didn't interest her now any more than they had then.

"You should have. Abigail has made you a wealthy woman."

"I was a wealthy woman before she died."

"Thanks to the Mahlers." This came from

Michael, who pursed his lips at the black driving gloves he was pushing on finger by finger. "Elizabeth and Anne are upset, and frankly I don't blame them. They have a point. That ring is worth a lot of money. You don't need the money, and you don't need the ring. It can't have anywhere near the sentimental value for you that it has for us." He raised his Mahler-blue eyes to hers. "If you're half the woman Abby always claimed you were, you'll give us the ring. It's the right thing to do."

Chelsea was thrown back in time to the parties her mother had given that the Mahlers had attended. Chelsea's friends had been impressed. They saw the Mahlers as jet-setters who hobnobbed with princes and dukes in the glitter capitals of the world and who spoke the Queen's English with flair. But Chelsea had never been charmed, then or now, by civilized speech expressing uncivilized thoughts.

She wanted to feel resentment or defiance but didn't have the strength. As with her inheritance, she had little taste for adversity in the shadow of Abby's death. "I can't think about this, I really can't," she said.

"If it's a matter of having the ring appraised," Malcolm suggested, "that's already been done. Graham has the papers."

"It's a matter of mourning. I need time."

"Don't take too much. The girls will likely go to court if you don't give up the ring on your own."

With an upraised hand, Chelsea murmured, "Not now," and took off for the kitchen. She was leaning against the center island beneath a tiara of copper pans when Graham burst through the door.

"Ahh, Chelsea," he breathed, "I was worried you'd left."

Chelsea liked Graham. A contemporary of her parents, he had taken over as Abby's attorney after his father died. Over the years he had been a quiet constant in her life.

Tucking her hands under her arms, she sent him a pleading look. "Don't you start in on me, too, Graham. It was bad enough reading the will while Mother's still warm in her grave, but to bicker over it is disgusting. They wanted it read, now it's been read, but I have no intention of looking at it, thinking about it, or acting on it until I've had time to mourn her." She tossed a hand toward the front of the house. "They're off to jet home and return to their lives as though nothing has changed, and maybe for them it hasn't, but it has for me, and it has nothing to do with inheriting whatever I inherited and being worth such-and-such more than I was before. I refuse to define my mother's life in terms of dollars and cents, so if that's what you're here to do, forget it."

"It's not," Graham said, and drew an envelope from the inner pocket of his suit jacket. "This is for you."

Warily she stared at the envelope. It was old

and worn. "If that's an ancient stock certificate, I don't want it," she said, though the envelope didn't look official by any measure. It was small in size, nondescript, and even from where she stood Chelsea could see that there was no return address.

"Go on," Graham coaxed, nudging it closer. "Abby wanted you to have it."

"Was this listed in her will?"

"No. It was a private matter, something between her and me, and now you."

Curious, Chelsea took the envelope and immediately noted its weight. There was something inside. She shifted it in her hand, then studied the address.

The ink had smeared what was an awkward scrawl to begin with, yet she made out her mother's name. She had more trouble deciphering the name beneath that.

Graham helped out. "It was sent care of my father. That's his office address. He was the lawyer who represented your parents in the adoption."

Chelsea had known that, but Graham's mentioning it out of the blue was startling. Her heart skipped a beat, then made up for it by starting to race. Her eyes flew to the postmark. It too had faded with age, but its print was more legible than the scrawl beneath it. The date was November 8, 1959, the place "Norwich Notch, New Hampshire?" she read.

"Nor'ich," Graham corrected.

"I was born there?"

"Yes."

She was stunned. Wondering where she'd been born was as much a part of her as celebrating her birthday each March. To have an end suddenly put to the wondering—to ask a question and receive a yes—was overwhelming. *Norwich Notch*. She held the envelope in her hand as though it were something fragile, afraid to move it, lift it, open it.

From across the room came Kevin Kane's somber voice. "What's that, Graham?"

Graham's eyes went from Chelsea's face to the envelope in silent urging. She swallowed, then turned it over, lifted the flap, and drew out a piece of tissue paper that was as worn as the envelope itself. It looked to have been unfolded and refolded many times. Setting it carefully on the counter, she unfolded it but again. Inside, attached to a threadbare ribbon that had once been red but had long since lost its sheen, was a heavily tarnished silver key. At least, she thought it was a key. Its bow was a miniature French horn with coils ripe for the gripping, but its blade was unserrated, nothing more than a thin tube half the length of her thumb.

An image flashed through her mind of the metronome that stood on the grand piano in her parents' living room. That metronome had been her nemesis through years of laborious piano lessons. It was wound by a key with a similarly smooth blade.

Bewildered, she raised her eyes to Graham's. "Who sent it?"

He shrugged and shook his head.

"*Is* it a key?"

"Abby thought so, but she never knew for sure. It arrived when you were five." For Kevin's benefit, he added an apologetic, "Since it was addressed to Abby, my father had no choice but to pass it on."

Chelsea followed his gaze. "There was no reason why he shouldn't have," she said to her father. His frame filled the doorway, stately in spite of his tired eyes and the weight that lay heavy on his shoulders.

"Oh, yes, there was," Kevin contended. His feelings on the subject hadn't changed over the years, not with Chelsea's reaching adulthood, not now with Abby's death. "You were ours from the time you were eight hours old. We raised you and loved you. Your mother didn't want to know where you'd come from. She didn't have to know it. That information was irrelevant. It still is. Everything that you are today came from us."

Chelsea knew what wasn't true. She had neither the purebred Mahler look nor Kevin Kane's grooved chin, thin lips, and ruddy complexion, and whereas both the Mahlers and the Kanes were musically inclined, she was tone-deaf.

But she wasn't about to argue with Kevin on that score. In the best of times he was threatened by the thought of her going after her birth parents, and these were far from the best of times. He was in pain. So was she, and his distance didn't help. She couldn't bear the thought of driving him farther away.

Nor, though, could she ignore the key. Laying it in the palm of her hand, she ran her thumb over it front and back. "Who sent it?" she asked again.

"Abby never knew," Graham said. "She received it exactly as you have it now."

Setting down the key, Chelsea flattened out the tissue paper and studied one side, then the other. Likewise she turned the envelope over and back. There was no writing other than what was on the front, no sign of a message. "There had to have been a note."

"She said there wasn't."

"She also said she didn't know where I was born," Chelsea blurted out, because the realization that Abby had lied to her stung. Even worse was the thought that Kevin knew more. Her eyes found his. "Did you know she had this?"

Slowly he shook his head. The measuredness of the gesture expressed his anger. "I'd have prevented it if I could have. She had enough to worry about without agonizing over a key."

Feeling an overwhelming sadness, Chelsea said, "There wouldn't have been any agonizing if she'd simply given it to me."

"If she'd done that, you'd have run off."

"Because of a *key*? I don't even know what it's supposed to unlock!"

"You'd have found out," he said gruffly. "That's your way. When you're curious about something, you follow it through." His tone mellowed. "It was one of the things your mother most admired in you. You had the courage that she didn't."

Chelsea was astonished. "She had more courage than any one of us."

Kevin remained mellow in memory's grip. "She didn't see it that way. She was bound by her family nearly as much as she was by her leg braces, while you broke free. You did the things she might have liked to have done. You looked for challenges and met every one. She loved the flower child you were, just as much as she loved the club swimming champ." His mouth went flat, his tone hard. "Anyway, that's why she must have agonized over that key. She knew that you'd have taken that curiosity of yours and run off in search of elusive parents who didn't want you in the first place."

"Unfair," Chelsea whispered, feeling a knot in her throat. She ached for Kevin, who was afraid that two others would usurp his and Abby's places in her heart. But she ached for herself, too, because the last thing she wanted to believe was that she was alive simply because abortion had been illegal at the time of her conception.

Turning the key in her hand, she said softly, "I wouldn't have run anywhere. I certainly wouldn't have hurt you and Mom. You're my parents. That'll never change." She so wanted him to understand. "It's just that I've always wanted to know about the other." It was a deeply emotional subject for her. She doubted anyone but another adoptee would understand the sense of rejection that came with having been given away at birth, the isolation she felt at family gatherings, the incompletion that nagged and nagged.

But this wasn't the time to piggyback one emotional subject on another. With care, she set the key in the middle of the tissue and folded the paper as Abby had apparently done so many times. She returned the small package to its envelope and slipped the envelope into the pocket of her silk dress.

Raising her head, she said to Kevin, "You're right. It's not important now." As though to show him that Abby did indeed live on through her, she turned to Graham with much the same poise that her mother would have shown in equally trying times and said, "Cook makes an incredible potted chicken. You'll join us for dinner, won't you?"

Kevin knew Chelsea well. She was indeed a doer. When her college grade point-average had been lacking, she'd won acceptance as a graduate student at Princeton by literally planting herself and an impressive portfolio in the offices of the Department of Architecture. When she'd decided that she wanted her first apartment to be something loftlike in ways that nothing in Baltimore was at that time, she had presented a schematic design to one of the city's hot real estate developers, with promise of free working drawings to follow if he would buy the building she had in mind and take on the project. When she'd found herself with two partners in a brand-new architectural firm, she'd designed a striking logo and sent handwritten letters to every prospective client she could find in her personal address book. Given that she'd grow up with frequent exposure to her mother's family contacts and her father's professional ones, that address book was expansive.

Her challenge now was the tarnished silver key. She tried to ignore it at first. It was a wedge between Kevin and her at a time when she could least afford one. But the key wouldn't be ignored, seeming to blare its silent presence from wherever she chose to hide it.

Likewise, the name Norwich Notch came to have a familiar ring. She wondered whether some mystical force inside her was connecting with her birthplace or whether she had simply said the name so many times now that it rolled easily through her thoughts. An atlas at the library told her that the town was in the southwestern corner of New Hampshire and had a population of eleven hundred. But she found no mention of it in other books through which she browsed.

She did find reference to it in the phone book for the Keene-Peterborough area. Among other listings were the Norwich Notch Town Clerk, the Norwich Notch Congregational Church, and the Norwich Notch Community Hospital, any of which might have information on her birth. So her reading told her, and she had read almost every major article on adoption, published in recent years. She knew about searches. They were done all the time in the enlightened nineties. Social workers leaned increasingly toward shared information between birth parents and adoptees. Open adoptions were in vogue.

She could pick up the phone and make a call. She could fly to Boston and drive north or fly to Manchester and drive west. She could drive all the way from Baltimore if she wanted it, but she didn't. She wasn't ready to do any of those things. Not so soon after Abby's death. Not with Kevin so sensitive. Not with the reality of Norwich Notch so new. She needed time to adjust to its existence.

The key, though, fast became an old friend. After holding it, turning it in her hand, studying it night after night for a week, she took out a jar of silver polish and, taking care not to wet the frayed ribbon, worked the cream between each of the miniature slides. With every bit as much care, she rinsed it and dried it.

Free of tarnish, the key was a beautifully intricate thing. It looped lyrically, with detailing that Chelsea guessed was exact. Though the slim blade extending from the mouthpiece was nicked at spots, the horn itself was in perfect condition. As she buffed its slides with the pad of her thumb, she fancied that a genie might appear in a puff of smoke and tell her everything she wanted to know. But the night was quiet, and she remained alone.

She had so many questions, so *many* questions—the major one being who had sent it and why. Thirty-two years was a long time. People died. Situations changed. Then again, she wondered whether the key wasn't as crucial to her search as the postmark. Norwich Notch. So familiar. It sounded rural and charming; it could well be dirt poor and depressed. She wasn't sure she wanted to find out which; she wasn't sure she could *resist* finding out.

Meanwhile, the lure of the key grew. The more she studied it, the more intrigued she was not by the perfection of is crafting, but by the irregularity of the nicks on its blade. They were signs of use—use by people somehow related to her.

She imagined many different scenarios, all variations of those she'd dreamed up as a child. Her biological parents were always poor but in love. In one instance they were teenagers, too young and frightened to keep her. In another instance her father was married to someone else but desperately in love with her mother. In a third instance her parents were married to each other, with seven children already and no possible way to support an eighth.

Chelsea dwelt on that last possibility for a long time, because the thought of having one sibling, let alone seven, excited her. She had always wanted a brother or sister. She had begged Abby for one. In time she'd accepted that one child was as much as a woman with two useless legs and dubious health could handle, but she didn't stop wanting a sibling. As she saw it, a sibling was tied to a person in a way that friends weren't. She had grown up with hordes of friends, but she missed that other, special relationship. There were times when she felt a distinct sense of loss.

During those times, more often than not she turned to Carl.

Don't Miss These Enthralling Novels by Barbara Delinsky, Available from HarperCollins

Variation on a Theme

When flutist Rachel Busek and rough-hewn private investigator Jim Guthrie meet, they quickly discover that they are the perfect complement to each other. But there are troubling pieces of her past that Rachel must uncover before she can trust herself to love Jim completely.

Gemstone

It has been eight years since Sara McCray fled her husband, Jeff, and an opulent but stifling life in San Francisco led by her domineering mother-in-law. Now Jeff has become his own man, but Sara must decide if she can risk heartbreak again to take a second chance.

The Carpenter's Lady

Writer Debra Barry and carpenter Graham Reid are two people seeking to forget their pasts. Debra moves to the country after her painful divorce and hires Graham to redesign her new home. But as the house comes together Debra and Graham start thinking of building a future.

A Time to Love

Arielle Pasteur flies to St. Maarten, to a villa on a private beach, looking for solitude. Instead, she finds herself sharing the hideaway with a man who gives the impression of being an overbearing, scornful egotist. Yet behind the facade lurks a gentleness that makes Arielle question whether it's solitude she really craves.

Rekindled

Here are two Barbara Delinsky novels in one volume. *The Flip Side of Yesterday* and *Lilac Awakening* are two of her favorite romantic stories. Revised by the author and republished by HarperCollins, these stories have been rekindled.

Sweet Ember

Stephanie Wright was a nineteen-year-old camp counselor when she met and fell in love with Douglas Weston, a devastatingly handsome, older tennis instructor. Eight years later Stephanie returns to the camp where she was loved and betrayed, and the truth of that long-ago summer comes to light.

A Woman's Place

Claire Raphael is stunned when, upon her return from a hectic business trip, her husband serves her with divorce papers. He takes the house and custody of the children, too. But Claire has had to fight for every success in her life, and she's not about to give up now.

Finger Prints

Carly is the name she was given by the witness protection program. Even with a new identity, however, she is afraid her enemies will find her. Ryan Cornell is a young attorney who is fascinated by this secretive woman. But Carly cannot so easily reveal herself to another, however great the temptation.

Sensuous Burgundy

Small town assistant DA Laura Grandine and big-city lawyer Maxwell Kraig face off in an explosive courtroom battle. Yet it is the first time either has met their match for wit or will, and neither can deny the power of their attraction.

Together Alone

Emilie, Kay and Celeste have been best friends forever. When their daughters go off to college, however, each mother must find herself as a woman again. Barbara Delinsky expertly interweaves their stories in a beautiful work that is at once moving, romantic and real.

Moment to Moment

From the first moment Russ Ettinger meets Dana Madison, he feels the overwhelming urge to protect her. But Dana has been protected all her life and is determined to be loved only as a strong independent woman.

A Woman Betrayed

With a twenty-year marriage, two terrific kids and a successful career, Laura Frye has everything she could ask for—until her husband mysteriously disappears. Laura maintains that Jeff would never leave voluntarily. But how well does she really know her husband? As Laura tries to hold her family together, what she finds is a strength she never knew she had and a love she thought she had lost forever.